Ranger's Rescue

The Rescue Rangers Book 1

Caitlyn Lynch

Shenanigans Press

Contents

Location

Guàlize is a fictional country, carved out of South America and made up of parts of Venezuela and Colombia. The map below gives an approximate location. The underlined place names are fictitious.

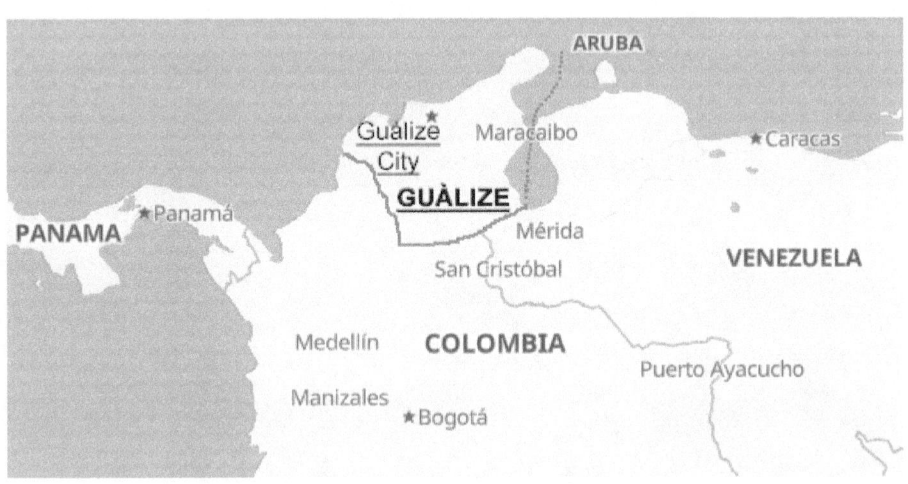

Chapter One

The hug was so tight Ariana almost choked. “Papi.” She patted her father’s back frantically. “I can’t breathe! Save me, Elliot!” she appealed laughingly to the head of her security detail.

Elliot only smirked at her, folding thickly muscled arms across his broad chest. “A father only gets to see his daughter graduate from medical school once. Plus, it’s been five months since he saw you at Christmas.”

Ariana rolled her eyes at Elliot over her father’s shoulder.

The hug eased, her father pulling back to rain kisses on her forehead and babble on about how proud he was of her. “My baby girl, a doctor.” Raul Monterro wiped at his eyes with a silk handkerchief plucked from the breast pocket of his bespoke Brioni suit. "How your mother would have loved to see this day."

The reminder made Ariana tear up too, and Elliot discreetly handed her another handkerchief. Her father embraced her again; this time she welcomed it, leaning into him as they shared a moment of still-aching grief.

"Please, sir," Elliot said after a few moments, his eyes never lingering in one place for long, "it's very exposed here. Let's get you both to the car."

"Of course," her father nodded, taking Ariana's hand in his and squeezing it as they walked together, surrounded by a phalanx of guards. "My baby girl, a doctor," he kept saying proudly.

Until Ariana laughed. "You know it will be five more years at least before I get board certification, Papi. Right now I'm only an intern."

"Are you not permitted to sign your name Doctor Ariana Monterro?" her father demanded.

"Well, yes," she conceded.

"Then you are a doctor," he declared with an air of finality.

Laughing at his determination to take full pride in her achievement and honestly feeling rather proud of herself in that moment, she slipped into the rear seat of the car beside him. Elliot drove, her father's own senior agent, Ramón Gutierrez, seated beside him with the others in a small convoy of cars around them. They were headed for the Guàlizean Embassy, of course. While Ariana lived in her own very comfortable apartment in Georgetown, her security team occupying the apartments on either side, having her father stay with her was out of the question. The Minister of Justice for Guàlize was too high-profile a target to risk at such a low-security location.

"Tell me how things are at home, Papi," Ariana requested as the limousine purred smoothly along. "It's been such a long time. Eighteen months," her tone was wistful. Even though her father came to the States three or four times a year and always made sure he carved time out of his busy schedule to spend with her, he always insisted Guàlize was too restless right now for her to come home.

“Good.” He nodded. “You read that we finally captured that idiot who was trying to incite a rebellion? Well, the movement fell apart without Duarte, and the countryside is peaceful again.”

“That’s wonderful, Papi!” She hugged his arm happily then put on her best hopeful look. “So, since my residency at Johns Hopkins doesn’t start for another six weeks, perhaps I can come home to visit for a while?”

He hesitated, shook his head with a regretful purse of his lips. “There are still threats, Ari.”

“There will always be threats. That’s why I have Elliot and my team, isn’t it?” She had long since accepted the necessity for her to live under high security and constant scrutiny. After her mother’s death, she welcomed her team’s devoted protection, but she refused to live in fear.

“You have to arrange the move into your new apartment…” Raul was losing the argument, and he was well aware of it as she gave him a direct look.

"Papi. I'm coming home. Once my residency begins, I'll be working eighty or hundred-hour weeks, and vacation days will be few and far between. I want to spend some time with you before that begins. It's been too long since I was home." She missed Guàlize desperately. While she had long since resigned herself to completing her studies and her residency in the United States, she still dreamed of one day returning home and applying her hard-earned skills as a doctor to improve the lot of her own people.

He sighed. "You'll let Elliot make the arrangements?"

He'd already acquiesced; she'd expected it to take several more minutes of wheedling. Ariana smiled, victorious, as Elliot glanced into the rear-view mirror and nodded, an assurance to her father that he would always ensure Ariana's safety.

"Of course, Papi," she said demurely. "Whatever you say."

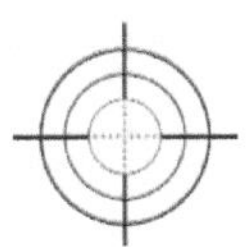

The travel arrangements included a private jet, as was standard. A commercial flight was out of the question, and certainly nobody outside a very small circle of trusted agents was aware that Ariana was going to Guàlize at all. Raul had arranged for two weeks of vacation from his governmental duties, and they planned to travel to their family's private estate an hour's helicopter flight from Guàlize City as soon as her plane arrived to enjoy a pleasant holiday in each other's company.

Clearly excited, Ariana kicked off her shoes as soon as they boarded the jet and had to be told three times by Elliot to sit down and fasten her seatbelt.

"I'd think you were sixteen, not twenty-six, if I hadn't seen how much knowledge you've crammed into your head in the last few years. Now sit down so we can take off!" He put a firm hand on her shoulder, pressing her down into her seat.

She smiled up at him, her brown eyes alight with excitement. "I'm just so excited to be going home, Ell!"

"I know." He settled into the seat opposite her and buckled his own belt. "But we've still got a five-hour flight to Guàlize City and then another hour in the helicopter, so settle the hell down or you'll drive me insane."

She laughed and obeyed, temporarily at least, until the jet had taken off and ascended to cruising altitude. Then she was up again, full of boundless energy to work off. She took long strides up and down the aisle, pausing to chatter excitedly with Emma, the only member of her security detail who hadn't yet visited Guàlize and was almost as excited about the trip as Ariana herself.

Elliot sighed and settled deeper into his seat, his eyes following Ariana fondly. She was like a younger sister to him, and his wife, Mara, mothered her incessantly, always encouraging her to eat better, get more rest. Thinking of Mara, he smiled quietly to himself. She hadn't been able to accompany them to Guàlize just now, as she was unable to get the vacation days from work, but she would follow in a week on a commercial flight. Raul was even lending them the Monterro beach house for a week-long getaway that

Elliot was looking forward to, knowing he could trust Raul's own highly-trained security team to protect Ariana just as fervently as he would himself.

"We must have champagne to celebrate!" Ariana declared then. "Tomàs, open a bottle — or two! Everybody should have some!"

Tomàs, a former FBI agent, looked to Elliot for confirmation. He glanced at his watch, smiled, and nodded. "Yes, everyone have a glass. It'll be long out of our bloodstream by the time we land."

There was a small cheer from the others of the detail, a small but fiercely dedicated team of men and women Elliot had handpicked. Tomàs grinned and nodded, heading for the back of the plane. He returned a couple of minutes later balancing a tray of filled champagne glasses like a professional waiter, handing them out to everyone.

"I forgot mine!" he said with a shake of his head, returned to the galley, and came back with one last glass. "To Ariana's homecoming!" he proposed, lifting the glass to his lips.

Ariana laughed merrily and took a long gulp of champagne, as the others echoed Tomàs' toast before joining him in drinking.

Tomàs drained his glass and set it down on a table. He leaned back against the bulkhead and folded his arms, watching the others as they sipped and talked, Ariana's happy laugh ringing out again as she answered Emma's questions about her homeland.

You're going home all right, princess, he thought privately. Just not in quite the way you expected.

It came on so gradually, a creeping sense of lassitude, that at first Elliot thought it was just his tiredness catching up with him. He'd had a long couple of weeks, making security arrangements for the trip, arranging for Ariana's move into her new apartment, plus doing some background checks on her future colleagues at Johns Hopkins. Setting his champagne glass down on the table between his seat and Ariana's, though, he was a little alarmed to find that he didn't seem to have any feeling in his hand. He watched with growing dread as the glass clanked hard on the surface, his hand no longer properly under his control.

Lifting his hand toward his face, it felt as though it weighed a hundred pounds; it took an immense effort. It took even more of his strength to turn his head and look at the others, to see Emma slumping back in her seat with her eyes closed, champagne spilling across her lap from her fallen glass. Ariana sliding bonelessly to the floor in the middle of the aisle, her glass shattering beside her.

"Drugged," Elliot managed to force out through a tongue that suddenly felt too big for his mouth. His eyes fell on Tomàs still standing, watching them with a sardonic smile on his face. "You."

"Me," Tomàs unfolded his arms and stalked forward with lethal grace.

“Why?” Elliot managed to gasp out with the last of his strength as Tomàs’ powerful hands clamped on the sides of his head.

There was no answer. Only a sickening crack and then blackness.

Chapter Two

Tomàs let Elliot's body drop from his hands then glanced around. Everyone else had succumbed to the tainted champagne sooner; Elliot was a big man and the drug had needed a little longer to take effect. Methodically, Tomàs moved through the cabin, repeating his murderous actions on each unconscious member of the security detail. As for Ariana, he lifted her away from the shards of broken glass onto a seat and left her there, slumped over. She'd remain unconscious for at least a few more hours, plenty of time for him to carry out the rest of his plan. Indeed, he hadn't intended to make his move quite so soon, but everyone having a drink at the same time was just too good an opportunity to pass up, especially since Ariana had fortuitously asked him to get the champagne. The pilots wouldn't come into the cabin to look for them; they were hired professionals who had orders to stay in the cockpit unless necessary. Still, Tomàs took the time to arrange everyone to look as though they were merely sleeping and kick the broken glass shards under a seat so they weren't immediately visible. Just in case. He was a meticulous man who didn't leave anything to chance.

Turning on his phone to check the time, he switched on the GPS function and brought up a map, checking their position. Plenty of time to wait; they were still flying over the United States — they hadn't even crossed from Georgia into Florida airspace yet. He poured himself a fresh glass of untainted champagne and settled into the seat opposite Ariana to sip on it slowly, mentally running through the steps he would need to take to complete his plans, considering every possibility that might prevent his success.

It was a little more than three hours later when his phone pinged softly, alerting him that the plane had passed a certain point in the southern Caribbean and it was now time to prepare for the last stage of his plan. Getting up, he moved steadily through the plane, collecting what he would need.

Picking Ariana's unconscious body up, he methodically stripped her of her clothes. She'd already removed her shoes, shoes he was well aware contained implanted tracking devices since he'd taken new pairs to the electronics shop which installed them. As far as he knew, the same precautions weren't taken with her clothes, but again, he didn't intend to take chances. Everything came off, including her watch and the small gold studs in her ears. Stripping the clothes off Emma's body, he put Ariana in those instead. Ariana was a couple of inches taller and Emma was more heavily muscled, but the simple outfit of black pants and blouse fit well enough. Emma's shoes were too small, though, so he left Ariana barefoot. He'd get shoes for her once they were on the ground.

Carrying Ariana to the rear door, he laid her limp form on the floor while he opened an overhead bin and took out a harness of straps and a packed parachute.

It was the work of a couple of minutes to attach the harness to Ariana. Leaving the parachute on the floor beside her, Tomàs made his way to the cockpit door, knocking firmly on it.

The door opened after a moment. “Señor Fuentes, que pasa?” the co-pilot said with a cheerful smile upon seeing him, half-standing in polite greeting.

“Just coming forward to see where we are, Esteban. Please, sit down,” Tomàs gestured with a smile, and the co-pilot nodded, turned his back, and began to ease back into his seat.

The man didn’t even have the time to process his imminent death as Tomàs’ knife slashed across his throat. Paulina, the pilot, glanced at them, her mouth opening to shout with horror — a shout that never sounded. There was only a horrible gurgle as Tomàs cut her throat open too, his heavy, razor-sharp combat blade parting skin and muscle like butter. The pilot’s eyes glazed over as her lifeblood spurted from her slit jugular, dead before she could even think of fighting back.

Ignoring the blood sprayed all over the instrument panels, Tomàs sheathed his knife and leaned forward. He'd undergone a solid week of training for this exact moment, knowing that he would have to perform a long sequence of complex commands from memory alone. He brought up the already-active autopilot and keyed in co-ordinates, overriding the automatic safety warnings that popped up. He murmured the rehearsed steps under his breath until, at last, he was certain the job was done correctly. Turning on his heel, he swiftly left the cockpit, leaving the two dead pilots slumped over in their seats as the plane turned onto its final course.

Moments later, Tomàs shrugged on his parachute and fastened the straps; lifting Ariana and attaching her harness to his front, he checked the GPS on his phone again.

Just a few more seconds... Now! Slipping the phone into a pocket and zipping it closed, he yanked the emergency release handle on the door. Instantly, the wind sucked hard at him, threatening to whip him and Ariana out into nothingness, but he was an experienced parachutist and had braced himself against the doorframe.

“Time to go, princess,” he said to the unconscious girl dangling limply in front of him and stepped out of the plane.

Tomàs saw the first flare go off in the jungle below even as he jumped; he grinned to himself. Perfect. There wasn’t even much wind today. Ariana’s unconscious dead weight made it hard for him to steer them in freefall, but he’d have plenty of time for that once he opened his ‘chute.

The parachute snapped open perfectly above him — of course it did, he’d packed it, and he was a professional. He’d enjoyed skydiving for years, even before he’d joined the FBI and later Ariana Monterro’s security team.

Grasping the handles of the parachute, he steered expertly toward the narrow black ribbon just barely visible between the trees rushing up to greet him. Getting caught up in the jungle canopy was not exactly the entrance he wanted to make, so he was careful to steer in between the high branches of the trees.

The black ribbon was a road, he knew. Had he been alone, he'd have made a perfect running landing, but with Ariana hanging unconscious beneath him, he couldn't do that. Nor did he want to drag her along the road's rough surface. He was being paid to deliver her in as perfect condition as possible, after all. So he hit the parachute release straps a few feet above the ground, grabbed Ariana up, and rolled himself around her in a tumbling fall which landed them in a tangle of arms and legs on the softer ground just at the edge of the road.

It was still the most uncomfortable landing Tomàs had ever experienced, and he lay still for a moment, sucking in a few deep breaths and carefully testing his limbs. Nothing broken, just a few bruises. Ariana was still out cold, and he couldn't find any obvious injuries as he crouched over her to quickly check her over. The rumble of an engine reached his ears, an old panel van stopped just a few feet away, but he didn't look away from his task. His new employer was an exacting man, and Tomàs was being paid to deliver Ariana Monterro in perfect condition.

“Hola, Señor Fuentes,” a voice said above him.

He looked up and smiled. “Hello, sir. I have your package.”

Chapter Three

"Personal phone call for you, sir," his secretary said as Captain Jack McAuley entered his outer office, still sweating from his morning workout. He'd shower and change in the small bathroom attached to his office before starting on the stack of paperwork he could see looming on his desk.

"Tell them I'll call them back." He couldn't think of anyone from his personal life who might need him for something that couldn't wait fifteen minutes while he had a shower.

"Sir... it's Mr. Savige's wife. She says it's urgent." His secretary was a smart young petty officer who knew when to interrupt him.

"Mara?" A chill settled over Jack, foreboding raising fine hairs on the back of his neck.

He stopped mid-stride on the way into his private office and blinked, surprised. Why would my best friend's wife be calling me at work? "I'll take it in my office."

"Yes, sir."

The line clicked as he picked up the phone on the desk in his small office, indicating that his secretary had hung up. "Mara? You there? It's Jack."

"Jack." Her voice was heavy with tears. "Oh, Jack..."

He knew at once; he'd heard that tone of grief too many times. "What happened?" he demanded. "Is Elliot all right?" He hesitated before forcing another name out. "Ariana?"

It had been six years since he'd laid eyes on her. Even though Elliot and Mara were very much part of her life, he'd carefully avoided any event where she might possibly be at, not so difficult since they'd moved to D.C. with Ariana and Jack still lived on the Ranger base at Fort Benning. Even so, at the slightest hint of trouble, his thoughts were of the woman who'd captured his heart and never let it go.

“The plane crashed, Jack…”

He couldn’t breathe. Ari. The thought of her dead, of her bright vitality snuffed out, was too much to bear. It took him several tries to get out the single word, “Where?”

“They were going to Guàlize, Ari was going to spend a few weeks with Raul after her graduation… I was planning to fly down in a few days, Raul had offered Elliot the beach house; we were going to take a vacation.” Mara was still crying, but it was slower now. “The President of Guàlize himself called and told me. Jack, I can't bear it. I can't… I can't get through to Raul and they want me to fly down and identify Elliot…”

“No.” Jack knew instinctively that Mara wouldn’t be able to manage that. Not even if Elliot's body was intact enough to identify, which having been in an airplane crash wasn't particularly likely. Especially not if the aircraft had burned. The thought of Mara faced with Elliot’s destroyed body was beyond unpalatable, so his reaction was instant, unthinking. “I’ll go, Mara. I'll bring him home.”

She sobbed with relief. “Thank you, Jack, oh God, thank you so much.”

“Are you alone? You shouldn't be...”

“No. No, I'm not alone. My sister's here with me. I'm going to go home with her for a while... you have my number.”

“I do. I'll call you as soon as I find him, Mara. I promise. I'll bring Elliot home for you.”

He stared at the wall dry-eyed for a full minute after Mara hung up, the receiver still in his hand, remembering his friend. The grueling days in Ranger School together when they'd competed jokingly against each other to be the best but still picked each other up when they'd felt they couldn't go another step. The even more grueling tours through the deserts of the Middle East and the mountains of Afghanistan. The firefights. The hasty sutures Elliot had put in a bullet hole in Jack's leg on a hellish mission in Somalia before they'd half-carried each other off the battlefield.

The good times. Standing beside Elliot as his best friend married his childhood sweetheart, just a little envious of the obvious love the couple shared. Grieving with Elliot after his friend drunkenly confessed one night that he was firing blanks, that he couldn't give Mara children. Laughing, but flatly refusing when Elliot asked him for a sperm donation. “Mara loves you, Ell. You don't need kids to be complete. Especially not a big cuckoo in the nest that any kid of mine would be. If Mara asks, I might say yes; otherwise, definitely no.”

Mara had never asked, which was how Jack knew it had been Elliot's idea and his alone. Mara had never needed more than Elliot's love to be happy.

And now she didn't even have that, the love of her life ripped away from her by a tragic accident, his body lying cold and ruined on some distant mountainside.

With Ariana's.

Jack's mind shied away from the thought. Pressing a button on his phone, he told his secretary, “Petty Officer Kowalski, get me Lieutenant Colonel Cullane at once, please.”

“I have him, sir,” Kowalski said a couple of minutes later.

There was a click on the line, and his commanding officer Brody Cullane's deep voice said, "Captain McAuley; what seems to be the problem? Your secretary indicated it was urgent."

"I've just had a phone call from Mara Savige, sir. Elliot Savige's wife? There's been a plane crash in Guàlize, and it seems pretty much certain that Elliot is dead."

Brody sucked in his breath. "Oh shit, Jack, I'm sorry." He knew all about the close friendship between the two men. "He's still working for the Monterro family?"

"Yes, sir." Jack's own indrawn breath was a little unsteady. "There's a high probability that Ariana Monterro has also been killed."

Brody was silent for a moment, and then he asked in a calm, formal tone, "What do you need, Captain McAuley?"

Jack let out a silent sigh of relief and leaned back in his office chair. "Mara Savige has asked me to go down there to identify Elliot's body and repatriate him. I'd like to request official leave to do so."

"Granted," was the immediate response. "I'll sign you off for a week right now; let me know if you need any more time than that. Do you want a team to take with you?"

"I shouldn't think so, sir," Jack said gratefully. "Unless," a sickening thought occurred to him, "unless it wasn't an accident. In which case, I think we should probably wait for an official request for help from the Guàlizeans anyway, if they choose to make one."

"I'll leave it to your judgment once you're on the ground. Please keep me apprised of the situation — and please convey my deepest sympathy to Minister Raul Monterro."

If he did that, it would be an acknowledgment that Ari was dead. Jack closed his eyes in grief. "Yes, sir," was all he said, though.

"Do you have transport?" Brody's tone became crisply efficient again.

"Not yet, sir. I was planning to head for the airport and get on the first flight that'll get me to Guàlize."

"I think we can maybe do a little better than a commercial flight, Jack. Let me pull a few strings. That way you can get to the crash site itself a lot faster without having to wade through miles of red tape. With any luck, I can get permission from the Guàlizeans for you to parachute in directly; that means you can go in uniform and armed, too. You'd be our official representative."

"I think the Ambassador might have something to say about that, sir!"

"Not the United States' official representative to the country, Jack." Brody snorted with laughter. "The Rangers' official representative to Raul Monterro, offering our assistance in whatever he needs. I can slide that nicely by the authorities, especially if you enter the country in uniform but not via the airport. We have enough history with Monterro, especially you personally, that I should be able to get the powers-that-be to sign off on it pretty quickly, and that means I'll be able to call in a few favors from the Air Force to get you a ride down there."

"I'll leave that to your superior ability to kiss ass, sir," Jack said in extremely polite tones.

Brody laughed. “Get out of here, Jack. Go get your kit together. And keep me in the goddamn loop.” He dropped back to a somber tone. “I’ll have Selina go see Mara Savige. Assure her that the Rangers are here for her even though Elliot died a civilian. You bring his body home so we can give him the send-off he deserves.”

“Yes, sir,” was all Jack could say. “Thank you very much, sir,” he added before putting the phone down and leaning back in his chair to press the heels of his hands hard against his burning eyes.

Brody called back two hours later on his personal cell. Jack was at home, preparing things for at least a week’s absence, getting his neighbor to pick up his mail, and emptying out his refrigerator. He’d already packed himself a parachute and a light pack with a couple of spare sets of fatigues. He wasn’t going to go in armed for war, but he planned to pack his personal sidearm and a couple of clips of ammunition, provided Brody could get him authorization to take them into Guàlize.

"Everything's squared away with the top brass," Brody came straight to the point. "I'm waiting on a call back from my Air Force counterpart, who's just arranging with the Guàlizeans when and where you'll be dropped. They're not talking about the crash to anyone; it's being kept very hush-hush for now."

That sounded fishy to Jack, and he immediately said so.

"You and me both," was Brody's response. "Ariana Monterro's a VIP down there by anyone's definition, considering that her father is almost certain to be the next President from what my source at the State Department told me. A plane crash involving her should be all over the news, but nobody at this end had any idea it had happened until I told them."

"I didn't know Raul Monterro was in line to be President," Jack said, startled.

"Neither did I, but State seem pretty sure. The Guàlizeans have a similar system to us; their president can only serve a maximum of two four-year terms. Word is that Raul is the heir apparent, and the election is less than two years away. Nothing is official yet, but his popularity with the general public, his good relations with the US, and his willingness to kick ass and take names against the drug lords should make him pretty much a shoo-in with the electorate."

Jack rubbed at his forehead, swearing under his breath. "This complicates things a hell of a lot more."

"No shit, Sherlock. I'll send your dress uniform down to the American Embassy in Guàlize City just in case you have to make any public appearances with Raul. State told me in no uncertain terms to make it very clear that Monterro, President Garcia, and the country of Guàlize have the full backing of the United States of America. They've got a team from the National Transportation Safety Board on standby to go down and assist with investigations, but the request will have to be made from that end. It'll be your call on the ground whether to press Raul to make that request, Jack, so keep your eyes open and your wits about you."

"Yes, sir," was the only possible response Jack could give to that instruction.

So here he was, several hours later, looking down on the jungle speeding by underneath the plane's belly, once again preparing to increase his ratio of takeoffs to landings.

"Ready, Captain?" the loadmaster shouted in his ear, and he nodded sharply, pulling his goggles into place. It wasn't a particularly high jump; they were only at fifteen thousand feet. He could see the mountain now, the huge gash ripped into the foliage by the doomed aircraft as it crashed through the thick jungle canopy. "Three, two, one, jump!"

Nobody survived that, was Jack's first thought as he freefell toward the crash site. The aircraft had broken up into half a dozen large pieces; he was somewhat surprised that there didn't seem to have been much fire, but then it had been less than a hundred miles from its destination at Guàlize City — probably hadn't had much fuel remaining in the tanks. The rainforest was thick here, plenty of regular precipitation. Maybe the foliage was wet enough that the fire hadn't had much time to catch hold. He popped his parachute canopy at the perfect moment and carried on surveying the crash site from the air as his freefall slowed to a glide.

Over there, he thought, that black stripe in the jungle is the sign of a fire. One of the engines perhaps, ripped free from a wing as the plane crashed through the tree canopy.

A lit flare caught his attention, and he turned his head, realizing that someone was trying to guide him in for a landing. There was a crosswind, but for an expert parachutist like Jack it was no problem to adjust his angle of approach and land where he was directed in the cleared gash on the approach to the wreckage.

"Captain McAuley?" the man who'd guided him in came hurrying up to ask in heavily accented English. "Minister Monterro is on his way."

"Thank you." Jack freed himself from the traces and picked up his pack, shrugging it onto his back. “Lead the way.” Nausea churned in his stomach as he followed the guide, the moment drawing ever closer when his nightmare would become all too real. He’d seen terrible things in war, but this wasn’t war… and Ariana Monterro had never been a soldier. She deserved so much better than a shockingly sudden end on this isolated jungle hillside.

Steeling himself for what he was about to see, Jack reminded himself that the man he was about to meet had lost everything. Ariana wasn’t just Raul Monterro’s only child, she was the only family the man had left. Jack owed Raul every ounce of professionalism he could summon up. Falling apart wasn’t acceptable, even though grief was tearing him apart inside.

Chapter Four

Raul Monterro has aged, was Jack's inconsequential first thought, as he recognized the man hurrying toward him, flanked by a whole phalanx of bodyguards. There were streaks of white at his temples, stark in his black hair, lines around his eyes that spoke of strain. But then, it had been six years since their last meeting, and what Monterro had been through in just the last few hours would have aged anyone.

“Sir.” He saluted formally. “Have they found her?”

Raul shook his head. “Not yet. We have Elliot’s body, though. I can identify him, of course, but since Mara wanted you to come...”

“I promised I'd bring him home,” Jack said simply.

Raul nodded in complete understanding. “This way.”

The plane's fuselage is surprisingly intact, Jack realized as he followed Raul, the phalanx of bodyguards eyeing him suspiciously. The plane hadn't crashed straight-on into the mountain as he'd first thought, but sideways along its flank, tearing out a thick swathe of foliage. The wings had come off first, the engines with them, a small fire burning out in the wet rainforest quickly and never reaching the body of the plane, which had cracked into three sections: nose, middle and tail.

“Jack,” Raul said quietly, “officially they're still calling it an accident, but there's something you should see.” He led Jack toward the nose section and the shattered cockpit door hanging loose on its hinges.

Looking at Raul's face, Jack knew at once that something was very, very wrong with the picture he was seeing. Shoving aside the crumpled door, he leaned into the cockpit and saw the two pilots still strapped in their seats, slumped forward over their instruments.

The blood staining their white shirts was almost black.

Long inured to the smell of death, Jack ignored it. Reached out to carefully tip up one of the pilot's jaws. His lips tightened at what he saw. His eyes met Ariana's father's, and he nodded to show Raul that he understood. Raul put a hand on his arm and indicated they should walk away from all the listening ears around them.

"Their throats were cut," Jack said quietly as Raul led him from the crash site, waving his bodyguards to give them a little space. "This was no accident."

"The others, Elliot included, all had their necks broken. I am confident that they all died before the crash — and this was found in the galley area an hour ago." Raul took a clear plastic evidence bag from his pocket and held it up to show Jack the contents: a broken glass vial with a label still clearly visible on it, holding some of the shattered pieces together.

KETAMINE.

Spots of rage swam in front of Jack's eyes. “Ari. This was done to take Ari. Who?” There had to have been someone else on board. A stowaway...

“In addition to Ari, the only body we haven't been able to find is Tomàs Fuentes. He was former FBI.” Raul's eyes glittered with the same rage Jack felt. “He took my daughter, Jack. They took her again.”

Jack breathed in. Out. Focused on the rhythm, trying to calm the instinctive, burning rage that bubbled up in his throat, strangling him. “Tell me about Fuentes. I don’t know him.”

“He'd been with us for two years.” Raul stuffed the evidence bag back into his pocket and clenched his fists. “He was completely trusted. I have my people going over his dossier with a fine-tooth comb again, but Elliot had already checked him out. There was nothing there to find. An exemplary record with the FBI, a Guàlizean grandfather who emigrated to the US way back in the sixties, he ticked all our boxes. Elliot wanted him for his profiling skills because of all the new people Ari was coming into contact with in her work."

"Sir!" a shout from behind them made them turn. One of the searchers was holding something up in gloved hands... something bright orange. "We've got the other black box, sir!"

"I know you've promised to take Elliot home to Mara, Jack, and I will make that happen as soon as possible. But please, I beg of you." Raul put his hand on Jack's arm. "Every single person I trusted with my daughter's life is now dead, except for one who has betrayed us... and you. Help me find her. Please."

"You should know that you don't even have to ask, Raul. I'll find her, and I'll get her back," Jack said through gritted teeth.

"Good. You will have everything you need, of course, every resource Guàlize has is at your disposal..."

"No," Jack said immediately.

"What?" Raul blinked.

"This needs to be kept quiet, Raul. Whoever did this went to a great deal of trouble and expense. The plane crash is a splashy, attention-grabbing stunt; whoever organized this wants attention, wants to know he's gotten under your skin. You mobilize the entire Guàlizean military, this is going to be all over the news. You'll be giving the kidnapper exactly what he wants."

Raul gazed up at Jack thoughtfully. "We need to give him what he wants in order to get Ariana back."

"I am one hundred percent sure that you will not be able to live with giving him what he will ask for in exchange for Ariana's life." Jack stared the older man down steadily.

Raul dropped his gaze then swore under his breath. "You're right. Dammit, you're right. And the more we splash this over the news and make a production over it, the more he knows he can demand, whoever he is. And he has an FBI-trained agent on his payroll, a man who knows the standard hostage negotiation tactics, knows exactly what the normal moves should be."

"We have to think outside the box to outwit Fuentes; we have to make the kidnappers come to us. So nothing on the news, Raul, no grieving father appealing for mercy. No acknowledgment that this plane crash even happened. Every single one of these people you have here needs to know that if they so much as breathe a word that this plane went down, they will have made an enemy for life of Raul Monterro."

"We make the kidnappers come to us," Raul repeated thoughtfully.

"Correct. That way, you're negotiating from a position of strength, even though they're the ones holding the aces. Or the queen, in this case."

"And you?"

"I'm the one tracking the bastards down and breaking all their necks with my bare hands for even thinking about taking Ari," Jack said, his eyes flint-hard with seething rage.

Raul smiled, showing his teeth. "I cannot tell you how glad I am you said that." Offering his hand, he clasped Jack's in a firm shake. "I'll handle the negotiating. You just kill the bastards and bring my daughter back."

Chapter Five

Ariana awoke with a hundred angry little men drilling behind her eyes. Groaning, she reached her hands up to cover them from the bright light shining on her face.

Something wasn't right. Lots of things. Too many things.

Focus!

The bed she was sleeping on felt too soft, and there was something curiously furry underneath her. Pushing herself up to a sitting position, she squinted her aching eyes open to look around.

"What the hell..."

She was in a completely unfamiliar room on a luxurious four-poster bed with gauzy drapes hanging at the sides. An ugly gilded mirror hung on the opposite wall, angled perfectly to reflect the bed, which made her grimace with distaste, even more so when she realized that the fluffy surface was real jaguar fur. She pulled her hands away from it in disgust. Real fur? Who would even consider such a thing?

Looking around, she saw open balcony doors; the afternoon sun that was slanting in through them had been the bright light that had landed on her face. There were tall trees visible outside the window and that was all wrong, everything about this room was all wrong. Including the clothes she was wearing, black pants and a blouse she didn't recognise and which didn't seem to fit her quite right. A pair of cheap jogging shoes had been crammed onto her sockless feet, making them sweat uncomfortably, but at least they seemed to be the right size, or close enough.

Pushing herself upright with another wince of pain for her pounding head, she headed over to the window to look out. She didn't get there, though; the door clicking open behind her made her whirl around.

"Tomàs!" she said with a gasp of relief. "Where are we? What's going on?" She looked behind him for Elliot, frowned to see that Tomàs was alone. "Where's Ell?"

"Elliot's dead, Ariana." His voice was flat and quite steady, his expression remote.

She sucked in a shocked breath and took a step back. "No. No, that's not possible." What the hell happened? The last thing I remember is... driving to the airport, actually. Glancing back to the window, she asked, "Where are we? Was there an accident?"

Tomàs nodded. "We're in Guàlize. You're the guest of my new boss. And I'm sorry about Elliot and the others, Ariana, but their deaths were necessary."

"You killed them," Ariana said in stunned realization, seeing the uncaring expression on his face.

Slowly, he nodded again. "I did."

She stood staring up at Tomàs in disbelief. He had the grace to look shamefaced, not meeting her eyes.

"Why?" was all she could think to say, in the end.

He let out a harsh little laugh. "Money, why else?"

Ari blinked and shook her head. "Tomàs, my father will pay you more for my safe return, you must know that..."

"Not even your father is rich enough to outbid El Lobo Negro, Ariana."

The name took her breath away. El Lobo Negro. The Black Wolf. Rumor said that he was a Colombian who had left the cartels of his own country and brought their brutal methods to Guàlize a decade ago, but if anyone knew his real name, they would not speak it. His alias and a blurry image headed her father's Ten Most Wanted list.

If Tomàs was working for The Black Wolf, if she was truly in the power of that monster, she wouldn't be returned to her father alive. Fatalistically, Ariana accepted the inevitable truth. After her mother's death, she'd made her father promise her, no matter what befell her, he would never put her safety above the needs of the Guàlizean people. He would never, ever negotiate with El Lobo Negro, not even for her sake.

“Take me to him,” she said, her head held high, though inside a part of her wept at the knowledge that she would never see her father again.

“You can shower and change first; there’s a bathroom over there,” Tomàs gestured. “And a wardrobe full of clothes, all in your size.”

“Which you provided to that murderous scum so he could obtain the clothes. How long have you been planning this, Tomàs? You didn’t even know I would be coming back to Guàlize until a few days ago.”

“We knew you’d come back one day,” Tomàs said with a shrug. “And this wasn’t the only plan to get you here, Ariana. Just the opportunity that presented itself soonest. Now why don’t you go take a shower?”

Her skin crawled at the very idea, because she’d just realized there had to be a camera in this room, that Tomàs and maybe others had been watching her sleep. How else had he known to come in when she’d gotten out of bed? And if there was a camera in this room, there would likely be one in the bathroom, too.

"You'd love that, wouldn't you?" she spat, rage and grief bubbling to the surface and pouring out in her words. "You want to go back to your monitor and jerk off watching me strip off my clothes and take a shower? No fucking way, you murdering bastard. I'd rather wallow in pig shit than give you the satisfaction."

He took a small step back, seemingly startled by her intensity. "There's no camera in your bathroom."

She didn't believe him. "Maybe not that you can see, you moron. Maybe it's for your boss's private entertainment. Well, I'm not putting on a show for him either." Ariana planted her hands on her hips and glared at Tomàs. "Take me to him. Now."

"You are not giving the orders here, princess!" he snapped back, expression twisting angrily. "I'm not being paid to cater to your every goddamned whim anymore. I work for El Lobo Negro now, and if he orders you stripped and whipped for behaving like the bratty, entitled little rich bitch you are, I will gladly wield the lash!"

She wasn't going to show fear, even though Tomàs was a big man and he was advancing toward her with clenched fists. Lifting her chin, Ariana looked him straight in the eye. "And what happens if you hit me now, Tomàs? Because my guess is that The Black Wolf has ordered me delivered in perfect condition. Touch me without direct orders, and it'll be you with the stripes on your back — that is, if he doesn't just shoot you in the head. I'm his bargaining chip, after all. You're just the hired hand who's already shown that he'll turn on his employer for enough cash."

Tomàs' expression darkened further, and for a moment, she thought he really might hit her. She held still, though, face turned up defiantly. This disgusting scumbag had killed Elliot, Emma, and her other friends. If he was stupid enough to hit her and get himself shot for it, well, that was one less problem she'd have to deal with. Tomàs knew her, after all, knew the way her mind worked. She was betting that nobody else here did, and that might, just possibly, play to her advantage if she was able to figure out some way to escape.

Tomàs Fuentes was a former FBI agent, though, and he was no fool, despite the rage and resentment fueling his actions. He stopped moving forward, instead glaring at Ariana for a moment before shrugging. “Fine. You want to go to him now, you go to him now. We’ll see how he deals with your disobedience.” He pointed at the door. “Now move, or I’ll put you over my shoulder and goddamn haul you down the stairs like a sack of flour.”

Ariana knew when to let him win a point. I’m definitely ahead in the mind games so far, she consoled herself as she moved toward the door with a slow, deliberate stride, her chin held high. She refused to even look in the mirror to see how messy her hair was. She wasn’t going to primp and preen for some kidnapping, murderous brute of a drug lord.

Tomàs making her go first was actually something of a blessing, because it meant he couldn’t see her eyes darting about, couldn’t see her taking everything in, noting every door, every passage that she would need to explore to find a possible escape route. They were obviously on the upper floors of what Ariana concluded was a very expensive — and extensive — house. Arriving at the top of a grand flight of stairs sweeping downward in an elegant curve toward a floor paved in black and white marble checks, she paused and glanced back at Tomàs.

“Down,” he ordered with a negligent flip of his wrist. She nodded and faced forward, placing her hand on the rail and descending slowly with her head held high, imagining herself at the Presidential Palace for a grand event while wearing a magnificent gown. The thought gave her strength, and as she reached the bottom, her jaw clenched with rage. Raul and Luisa Monterro’s daughter wasn’t going to cringe and grovel and beg for her life, not today.

Not ever.

Stopping at the foot of the stairs, she glanced around, seemingly casually, but in reality taking in every detail of the grand hallway.

Standing beside large, barred double doors was the first other person she’d seen in the house, a whip-thin, mustached man who stared at her, eyes running lasciviously up and down her body. Ariana stared back, head held high, her eyes spitting sparks, until the man glanced away.

I will not be cowed. I will use every weapon at my disposal to defeat these pigs.

"Over there," Tomàs touched her shoulder, pushing her lightly toward a door near the back of the hallway. She turned her glare on him, and he dropped his hand away as though she had burned him.

She took her sweet time before she moved again, but when she did, she marched swiftly away from Tomàs, grasped the door handle, and shoved the indicated door open without bothering to knock. She heard both Tomàs and the other man gasp behind her and smiled a tiny secret smile to herself. Another small victory; she was betting that nobody ever walked in on The Black Wolf without knocking.

The room beyond the door was dark with heavy shades over the windows drawn even in the middle of the day. It took her eyes a moment to adjust, but then she strode forward to the middle of the room to confront the man who had risen from a chair to face her.

“The Black Wolf, I presume?” she said coolly.

Chapter Six

Jack and Raul listened to the black box recordings, grim-faced. The cockpit recording had perfect clarity, no need for technical wizardry to clean it up. Everything seemed normal until about thirty minutes before the expected landing time, which tied in neatly with the crash site location.

The pilots had just been handed over from Dominican to Guàlizean air traffic control when there was a knocking sound, and: "Señor Fuentes, que pasa?" the co-pilot said inquiringly before there was a gurgling noise and then a cut-off shout.

The only sound after that in the cockpit was the sound of someone tapping keys; reprogramming the autopilot, they already knew, overriding the safety parameters. Fuentes had no formal pilot training according to his files. Someone had coached him very carefully in what to do to convince the jet to crash itself.

The cockpit door clicked shut. Just over nine minutes later the recording abruptly cut out, indicating the time of the crash.

"That ties in with this point in the electronics signals to the cockpit, sir," the air safety investigator who was assisting them pointed out to Raul. "See here?" He laid down a sheet of paper with time stamps down the left side with various codes Jack didn't understand next to the time notations. The investigator pointed to two time stamps in the center of the sheet. "This time here is when the cockpit door closes. Forty-eight seconds later, here," he jabbed the paper, "there's an electronic alarm signal that one of the aircraft's rear doors opened."

"That's Fuentes opening the door to make the parachute jump. It has to be," Raul said. "And he wouldn't linger in an open doorway at that altitude for more than a few seconds, not alone and presumably with

Ariana unconscious and strapped to him. He jumped pretty quickly after that, I'd say."

"That gives us a time stamp," Jack muttered, turning to look at the map spread out on the table. The jet's known flight route was drawn across it as a thick red line, the times and locations when it was picked up on radar carefully noted. The final location of the crash site was marked with a large red X he was trying not to look at.

"Somewhere midway between here and here." Jack picked up a blue pen and circled two radar stamps. He looked at the investigator's marked timeline, grabbed a ruler, and marked with an X the approximate point at which the rear door had been opened. "Give it, say, twenty seconds max before he jumped."

Marking a second point, he drew an elongated oval shape between the two. "They were still pretty high. About twelve thousand feet. That means the parachute drop was somewhere within this area." Fifty to sixty miles from the crash site, he figured. Far enough away that Fuentes wouldn't have to worry about tripping over emergency services rushing to the scene or investigators scouring the area while he made his getaway to wherever he was headed. Because if there was one thing which Jack was quite certain of, it was that Fuentes hadn't parachuted to his intended final destination. A FBI-trained agent would be far too smart to do something so easily tracked. No, the dropzone was just a waypoint Jack needed to check out on the path to finding Ariana.

The investigator nodded. "You're probably correct, sir." He checked the coordinates and pulled out a larger-scale map. He re-drew the oval on it before the three men bent over it.

"There's nothing here," Jack shook his head. "Just jungle."

"We need satellite imagery. I could make the request, but... it might be quicker if you did." Raul glanced at Jack. "The CIA or NASA are most likely to have the images we'll need at a useful quality. I'd have to go through government channels to get them, and it may take some time."

"Let me make some calls. I need to check in with Colonel Cullane anyway. He's already pulled strings to get me down here so quickly; he might be able to pull a few more."

Raul handed him a prepaid cell. "Untraceable. I promise."

"Thanks, Raul." Jack took the phone and moved across to the other side of the room to make the call, leaving Raul and the investigator still bending over the map, checking and double-checking the rough-and-ready calculations Jack had made.

"Cullane," Brody answered the phone with his customary quick snap.

"It wasn't an accident. Ariana Monterro has been kidnapped, and one of her bodyguards, Tomàs Fuentes, was almost certainly in on it," Jack came straight to the point.

"Bastard!" Brody growled furiously. "I don't recognize the name; was he one of ours?"

"Former FBI. Raul's got his people going over Fuentes' records with a fine-tooth comb right now, but my bet is it's going to come down to the usual motive."

"Money," Brody sighed. "All right. Elliot Savige?"

"His body's been recovered." Jack's throat tightened, but he couldn't allow himself the luxury of time to grieve. Not right now. Not when every minute meant another minute Ariana was in the hands of people who would murder six innocent people and crash a plane just to get their hands on her. Jack needed to focus. There'd be time to grieve later, he hoped. "And two other former Rangers. Raul's people are making the arrangements, and I'll accompany them back to the US as soon as I've recovered Ariana."

"Good. What do you need, Jack?"

Thank God for Brody's calm directness, Jack thought as he gave the coordinates for the satellite photographs they'd need. Brody told him that he'd call back as soon as he had them, and Jack hung up, never doubting for a moment that his superior officer would get the job done.

Two hours later, Jack lounged in a Guàlize City park alone on a park bench, wearing civilian clothes hastily sourced by Raul's secretary. Sipping on an iced fruit drink he'd bought from a nearby vendor, he looked as though he hadn't a care in the world and was just watching the brightly colored tropical birds flitting among the nodding palm trees in the warm afternoon breeze.

About five minutes after he sat down, a tanned, local-looking man sat down too, setting a folded newspaper down between the two of them on the bench.

"These didn't come from us," the man said softly in locally-accented Spanish, his lips barely moving.

"Muchas gracias," Jack said quietly in return, picking up the newspaper and ambling away. He could feel the envelope of stiff paper tucked in between the softer newsprint pages, but he wasn't rookie enough to take it out here and now. That could wait until he was back in Raul's office, away from prying eyes.

The photographs weren't the unbelievably high-definition ones Jack had seen used when planning field operations in Afghanistan and other trouble spots, but then again the US military still liked to pretend they weren't quite that capable, at least to foreign government officials. The images were still more than good enough for his purposes. An unsigned note tucked into the envelope apologized that there were no satellites in position for imagery at the time of the plane crash, but they'd provided some from a pass about two hours later.

“This is a road,” Raul murmured in a surprised tone, tracing his finger along the thin dark line winding between the trees. It wouldn’t have been visible at the standard resolution; certainly they hadn’t seen it when they’d taken a look at the available images on the Internet. “And a paved one, at that, except here and here, at the ends, do you see?” He pointed at two spots on the map, his eyes widening as he did so. “Madre de Dios, those bastards have built a paved road out here to facilitate their movements, and the government knew nothing of it! It cuts — maybe thirty miles off a journey between

San Cristobàl and Tierra Verdes, thirty miles of bad road that takes at least an hour to traverse!" He turned away from the map and paced up and down the office, slamming his fist against his hand. "No wonder we could never catch up to them, never figure out how they were getting their filthy product from the highlands down to the ocean!"

Jack let him pace and curse for a minute before calling his attention back to the photographs. "Raul. Raul, look." Carefully, he compared the satellite photos with the map, transposing coordinates and sketching the road onto the map with a pencil. "Look, the road goes right through the projected landing zone."

"It was all pre-arranged," Raul spat furiously. "Fuentes knew exactly when and where to jump. No doubt they were picked up and on their way before the plane even crashed."

Jack nodded; he'd already surmised as much. "And long gone before this satellite pass. But the question is, which way did they go?"

There were no vehicles along the length of the secret road on the photographs they had, but several traveled on the larger roads it eventually connected with in both directions.

"Down to the coast, or back up to the mountains," Raul mused. "That all depends on who took her, doesn't it?" He shared a dark look with Jack. The more time that passed without a demand for ransom, the more concerned they both became.

"Sir," Gutierrez, Raul's chief bodyguard and the only other man Raul trusted in the room with them right now, stood up from the desk, his bearded face pale. "Sir — an email just arrived!"

Chapter Seven

He's younger than I expected, was Ariana's first thought upon meeting the man who she was sure would kill her. He couldn't be all that much older than Ariana herself, mid-thirties perhaps, and tall and handsome. Though, as he stood to smile at her, she saw that the smile didn't reach his eyes, flat and dead as a shark's.

"Miss Monterro. May I call you Ariana?" he said politely in Spanish, moving around his desk toward her and extending his hand. His accent wasn't Gualizean, she noted at once, definitely more Colombian, which would give credence to the rumors about his origins — except he didn't look Colombian, either. Because The Black Wolf was white. Blond-haired and blue-eyed, freckles scattered across his pale skin. A tattoo peeping above his shirt collar, she couldn't quite make out what it was, sharp-tipped and angular.

What the hell is this?

"No." Her tone was flat and cold, her expression scornful as she ignored the offered hand. She had no intention of pretending civility, cooperating with whatever plans he had in mind, or making things easy for him by being docile and easy to manipulate. If she was to die, she'd die defiant, on her own terms, unbowed.

The Black Wolf blinked. "I see," he murmured. He studied her for a long time, but she refused to grow uncomfortable. Instead, she looked around the room, her head held high, disdain in her gaze as she noted the expensive artworks cluttered together, the gilded decorations, the tastelessly ornate furniture. Money but no class, she thought. Like so many of his kind, he desires legitimacy. Well, he will not get it from me.

"You may call me El Lobo," he broke the silence first, which she counted as a small victory.

"I think not," she responded in the same icy tone as before, ignoring him as she studied a small painting she thought might be a genuine Renoir... and one which she was sure she had seen on a list of famous stolen masterpieces.

He laughed, moved up behind her quickly, and grasped her elbow. Jerking it from his grasp, Ariana whirled on him, her eyes flashing. "Do not touch me!"

"You are quite magnificent, even more beautiful than your pictures," El Lobo said admiringly. "Perhaps you will call me Gustav, then."

"Perhaps I will call you Asshole. Kidnapper. Murderer. Monster!" she snapped back, repulsed at the thought of being on a first-name basis with the man who had ordered the murder of her friends.

"You would be wise not to antagonize me, Ariana," he said warningly. "At the present, you are an honored guest here. That can change at any time."

"Fuck you!" she snarled. "My father will never cooperate. Never. And neither will I!"

He scowled at that. "Oh, I think your father will do exactly what he's told, unless he wants to receive you back one piece at a time."

"That's what you'll have to do, then. Hey. Why don't you start with this one?" And, deliberately provoking, she held out her right hand — and flipped him the bird.

The Black Wolf's eyes widened with incredulity before he suddenly let out a great roar of laughter. She held still, hand out, finger upraised, until he grabbed it in a terrifyingly strong grasp, twisting her arm up behind her back painfully, too quick for her to fight back in any of the self-defense moves Elliot had so painstakingly drilled her in.

"Oh," he whispered in her ear as she struggled and swore at him, "you really are a feisty one. A shame to permanently mar something so lovely as yet, when we do not even know if your father is as strong as you hope. Let us, instead, take something that will grow back."

In the corner of her vision, she saw something glint and tried to wrench her head away, but the grip he had on her wrist was too tight, too painful. She could hardly move. Instead, she watched in despair as the sharp scissors snipped closed, shearing off a thick swathe of her hair at the left side of her head.

"Perfect." He let her go, and she sprang away, nursing her aching wrist and numb shoulder. He smirked at her, bending to pick up the hank of hair. "Tomàs, the camera. Smile for Daddy now, Ariana."

Of course, she wouldn't, twisting away and fighting to escape him, trying to keep her face turned away from the lens. They ended up with his strong hand around her throat, forcing her up on tiptoe with her face toward the camera as he held her freshly sheared hair up beside her face. Tomàs snapped half a dozen photographs before The Black Wolf let go of her. Ariana was certain there were bruises springing up on her throat to match the ones she could already see forming on her wrist.

“Take her back to her room while I make arrangements for the delivery,” he ordered, turning away.

Heedlessly, in a frustrated rage, Ari struck out, aiming a vicious punch at his kidneys with her unhurt left hand. Elliot would have been proud of her, she thought, as The Black Wolf went down with a yell. She followed up with a kick that would have broken his jaw if she'd fully connected. But Tomàs had already sprung into action, knocking her aside, tripping her with a quick leg sweep that made her stumble before she managed to regain her balance.

The Black Wolf leapt to his feet almost instantly, teeth bared, yanking a gold-plated pistol from under his suit jacket and pointing it at Ariana.

She faced him defiantly, shouting, “Do it! Do it, you monster, kill me!”

Slowly, he lowered the gun before smirking and putting it away. “No. No, pretty one, far better to teach you your lesson slowly. I have learned mine; I will not turn my back on you again. Not, at least, until your spirit is broken.

Take her away," he nodded to Tomàs, whose hand fell heavily on Ariana's shoulder.

She shrugged it off with a hiss of rage and a flash of her eyes. "Don't you dare touch me, you murdering piece of shit."

Tomàs' face darkened, his fists clenching.

"Miss Monterro is correct; you will not touch her except on my orders," The Black Wolf said unexpectedly. "Nobody touches her unless I say so. Is that clear?"

"Yes, sir," Tomàs said deferentially after a brief pause. "Do we summon you if she refuses an order, then, sir?"

"Yes, certainly." He smiled, an icy, triumphant smile, looking Ariana up and down slowly. "I am quite looking forward to teaching you the price of disobedience, Ariana."

She couldn't suppress a shudder of revulsion at the lecherous look on his face. He saw it and smiled wider, though the smile still never touched his cold eyes.

Whipping around, Ariana strode to the door. Let them think she was afraid and fleeing The Black Wolf's company; she fully intended to use the few seconds head start she was about to buy to do a little exploring.

She ran fleet-footed up the stairs before Tomàs even exited the study. Deliberately taking a wrong turn instead of going back to her room, which she was pretty sure faced the front of the house, she ran down the hallway leading in the other direction. Ariana could look out the front side later. Right now she wanted to look around and scope out the lay of the land as much as possible before Tomàs caught up with her.

Ariana hissed with pain as she hastily grabbed the first door handle she came across; her right wrist hurt like hell, already swelling up. Gingerly, clumsily, she used her left hand to try again, but the door was locked. She went onto the next as quickly as she could; locked.

"Fuck," she hissed under her breath. What kind of paranoid bastard locked all the doors in his house?

"Your room is this way," Tomàs' voice was dust-dry behind her. "It won't do you any good, Ariana. El Lobo knows you're not stupid. There's nowhere to escape to."

"Then you won't mind if I keep on looking around, will you?" She didn't bother looking at him, just marched on to the next door and tried that one too. It opened, rather to her surprise.

"I'm sure El Lobo won't mind if you want to wait for him in his bedroom, but I rather thought that was something you wanted to avoid." There was a nasty, knowing laugh in Tomàs' voice.

Ariana took a slow breath, mentally counted to five, and stepped back, closing the door again. Turning to face him, she said coldly, "Have you always been this much of an asshole?"

He's certainly not in control of his temper, Ariana thought as Tomàs' expression darkened again. Maybe he was always this angry, and now he no longer bothers to hide it... that was a depressing thought she tried hard to suppress as she walked back past him in the direction she knew very well her room was in.

“I’ll need ice and bandages for my wrist,” she threw over her shoulder. “Anti-inflammatories, too, if you have any.”

“He hurt you?” Tomàs was following her.

“Don’t even begin to pretend you give a damn,” Ariana snapped, “considering that you will have to help him cut off a lot more than just my hair in the days to come. We both know my father is never going to give El Lobo what he wants.”

“You’ll be the one to pay the price,” Tomàs pointed out.

“I watched my mother pay the ultimate price for no better reason than to buy me a few more minutes of time, asshole.” She shoved the door to her room open, turned around, and glared at him. “I’m not afraid. Or do you think it’s only men who can face torture and death with courage? Go and get me some ice and bandages.”

Slamming the door in his face gave her a great deal of satisfaction. She stood with her hand against the timber for a few moments, breathing quickly but quietly, until she heard his footsteps recede down the corridor.

Five minutes. I just bought myself five minutes… turning away from the door, Ariana stumbled over to the bed and collapsed on top of it, huddling down into a tiny ball. If I'm lucky, nobody is watching…

Her heart slammed against her ribcage, sweat beading on her skin as the first flashback hit.

Chapter Eight

"Sir — an email just arrived!" Gutierrez instantly had Raul and Jack's full attention.

"What email?" Raul demanded.

Gutierrez shoved himself up from his seat at the desk, pulling the laptop around with him. "It purports to be from the kidnappers, sir. There's a photograph attached."

"Don't look, Raul, let me..." Jack held out a hand to stop Raul.

"She's alive, sir, and she appears to be unharmed," Gutierrez said hastily.

"Show me," Raul demanded, with a nod to Jack to move aside. They both looked at the screen as Gutierrez brought up the image.

Ariana was glaring furiously at the camera, lips parted to show her gritted teeth. A powerful hand clenched on her throat was holding her chin forced up so that she faced the camera; another hand held a dangling hank of shorn hair at the side of her face. The ragged line where the hair had been cut showed very clearly.

Raul's jaw clenched with rage, but there was pride in his voice as he said, "She will not be cowed, my Ari. They will not break her."

"You're a fool if you believe that," Jack's voice cracked as he looked at the screen. "Anyone can be broken, Raul. Anyone."

Gutierrez shot him a look of dislike, but Raul held up a hand to silence him. "This is not the Rangers, Jack. Ari only has value to them as a hostage if they keep her alive and in good condition."

"You don't get it, do you?" Jack rounded on him, agony breaking the leash on his tongue. "That chunk of hair is going to turn up here in an envelope, tomorrow at the latest, with a list of demands. Every day that you don't meet them, another piece of Ari is going to turn up in a parcel. And it's not her they're trying to break, Raul. It's you."

He turned away, unable to look at either Raul or that image of Ariana anymore. The sure and certain knowledge that he would never see her alive again, that her kidnappers were even now considering which body part to cut off her first, ate at his insides like acid. Striding across the office to Raul's private bathroom, he shoved the door open before slamming it behind him, bending over the toilet and retching his guts up.

Raul was alone in the office when Jack came back out.

"Where's Gutierrez?" Jack asked.

"Tracking down some information for me. So, you're in love with my daughter."

Jack froze mid-stride, wondering what the hell he'd done to give himself away — and then realizing that even if the older man had only been fishing before, his reaction had just confirmed Raul's suspicions.

Raul nodded. "I wondered, six years ago. Since you haven't laid eyes on her from that day to this, as far as I know — and I know very well, thanks to Elliot — I can only conclude that you were doing your best to be honorable."

Jack had no idea what to say. 'I never laid a finger on her' would be a lie, plain and simple, and Raul had caught him with his guard well and truly down, so he just stood there and eventually shrugged. "She was never meant for the likes of me. I'm only a soldier."

Raul's eyebrows lifted, and then he snorted derisively. "You never met my wife. Luisa would have slapped your face for saying something stupid like that, but then she always liked to over-dramatize everything. She was an actress, you know."

Jack blinked, surprised. "I didn't know that, no. Was she a big star, here in Guàlize?"

"No. She was an extra. Hired to stand in the background a lot. Oh, she had dreams, of course, wanted to make it big. I was still practicing law when we met, a deputy district attorney with a fierce desire to clean up my country. She had witnessed a sanctioned drug killing while attending a party. An assassination, in other words." Raul's eyes glazed over as he reminisced about the love of his life.

Jack stayed silent, listening, wondering what Raul was trying to tell him.

"Luisa was afraid to testify. Everyone was afraid of the drug cartels then in Guàlize, even more so than today. I could not promise her that I could protect her; she knew that it would have been a ridiculous lie if I had tried." Raul shook himself out of his reverie and looked straight at Jack. "I fell in love with her the first time I saw her, Jack. I did something I've never done before or since; I told a witness to lie on the stand. I told Luisa to say that she couldn't remember what she saw, or to mis-identify the killer, anything to stop the cartel from coming after her. The thought of her dead crucified me, and I'd only spent a few minutes in her company."

Jack found himself unable to speak as Raul's eyes pinned him in place.

"Luisa told me later that she went away and researched me, asked all over her neighborhood what sort of man I was. She heard only stories of a fair man who fought like the devil to put away the guilty but would not prosecute when there wasn't enough evidence, a man who would not take payoffs, could not be bought."

"She must have wondered why on earth you told her to lie," Jack realized.

"She went to her church and she prayed to God to tell her what to do. And when the trial came, she looked the assassin straight in the eye and identified him as the man she saw pull the trigger."

Jack shook his head wonderingly. "She trusted you to protect her anyway."

"No, Jack, she didn't. She told me that I could not hope to win the war I was fighting if nobody would take up arms beside me. 'I am a daughter of Guàlize,' she said, 'and if I die to protect her, I will call it a life well spent.'" Raul turned, walked to his desk, and picked up the silver-framed photograph of his wife that always stood where he could see it. "Luisa put herself in harm's way several times over the next few months, making herself into a tempting bait as she worked with the police and my office, knowing that the cartel would not stop coming after her until they were broken, until they were on the run with far bigger things to worry about than one witness who would not keep her mouth shut."

"She must have been one hell of a woman," Jack said with deep respect in his tone.

"Oh, she was. She was." Raul smiled fondly at the photograph before setting it down. "But when I married her, once I was promoted to District Attorney after she helped me prove that my boss was taking money from the cartel, the press still said that she was 'only an actress.'"

Jack finally realized where the story was leading. He opened his mouth, not even sure what he was going to say, but Raul kept on talking right over him.

"So don't you ever say to me again that you're 'only a soldier.' I'd be very proud if my daughter married a man like you, Jack McAuley. There is no one, and I mean no one,

I would trust more to get her back for me. I'd have said that even before I was sure how you felt about her, by the way."

"I can't promise I'll get her back," Jack found his voice again at last. "That would be as much of a lie as if you'd told Luisa you'd protect her from the cartels. But I can promise you that I will goddamn well die trying, if that's what it takes."

"I know you will," Raul said simply before turning back to his desk. "You did not hear all of what the email gave us. It is signed with the name El Lobo Negro."

Jack had heard the name before. El Lobo Negro was a shadowy figure, but he'd still managed to get himself on any number of Most Wanted lists. Startled, he followed Raul to the desk and leaned over to look at the computer. "Do you have any way to confirm that?"

"No, but I cannot think of anyone else who would have the resources in Guàlize — and the sheer gall — to pull this off. I have Gutierrez looking up everything we have on

The Black Wolf's activities within a hundred miles of the landing spot."

"Do you want me to ask the same question of US intelligence?" Jack asked.

"I am placing this investigation in your hands, Jack," Raul said quietly. "You know better than I whether your country might have any information that could help us. I do not care what you have to do, who you have to ask, what favors you must promise; I will back you every step of the way. Guàlize's resources are at your disposal. Just bring my daughter home."

"This is a very great trust you place in me, Raul," Jack said after he caught his breath.

"Who can I trust more to bring Ariana home than the man who loves her?" was Raul's parting shot as the phone on his desk rang and he picked it up. "Buenas tardes," he said, gesturing at Jack to take the laptop and go across to the table and chair on the other side of the room.

Raul was carrying on a rapid conversation in Spanish with someone named Carlos; Jack did his best to tune it out, sitting down with the laptop and reading the email through thoroughly. The picture of Ariana had been closed down, which was a relief; he wasn't sure that he could have looked at it again just now without breaking down.

The attached email was in Spanish, of course, but he'd spent enough time studying the language to puzzle it out.

'I am sure you have realized by now that your daughter is not dead, Minister Monterro; she is a guest at my home and will be well-treated so long as you comply with my requests. The first request will be delivered along with the proof of your daughter's life tomorrow.'

It was signed, as Raul had said, El Lobo Negro.

Jack was quite sure that Raul had ordered Gutierrez to get people to work on tracing the source; he was equally sure that the NSA could do the same thing faster. Swiftly, he forwarded the email to Lieutenant Colonel Cullane, adding a note. 'I'm hoping that someone at the NSA owes you favors too, Brody. We need to find this guy ASAP. Jack.'

The click of Raul setting the phone down made him look up. Raul was looking at him with a half-smile on his face. “It seems you won’t be needing much Guàlizean help, Jack.”

“What do you mean?”

“You have some visitors.” Raul went to the door and opened it, gesturing. “Come on in.”

Three men in civilian clothes walked in, all of them grinning when they saw Jack. Out of uniform, they did not salute, but they all nodded respectfully before one of them said, “Good to see you, Captain.”

“What the hell are you doing here, Hunter?” Jack said in astonishment, getting to his feet.

“We’re on vacation, sir,” Hunter said blandly.

“On vacation — here. Right when Ariana Monterro’s been kidnapped,” Jack said incredulously.

“It’s a real coincidence, isn’t it? Heard you could maybe use some help.” Hunter shrugged. “Thought we’d stop by.”

“Colonel Cullane sent you, I dare say,” Raul said dryly.

All three men gave him innocent looks. “Don’t know what you’re talking about, sir. We’re on vacation,” Hunter repeated, obviously hellbent on sticking to his utterly implausible story.

“This is Lieutenant Hunter, Sergeant Mostyn, and Sergeant Diaz, sir,” Jack gave up and introduced them.

“I’m glad to meet you all, gentlemen,” Raul said. “And I’m glad that Captain McAuley will have the experienced assistance he needs. Gutierrez will get you anything you need, Jack,” he added. “Just say the word and it’s done.”

“Where are you going, sir?” Jack asked as Raul headed for the door.

“I have to brief the President on the situation. I’ll be back in an hour. And yes, I am quite safe in the Presidential Palace, thank you very much, gentlemen,” he added as Hunter and Diaz both glanced at Jack before taking a step in Raul’s direction. They both looked around, trying to appear innocent, not at all as though they’d intended to follow him to ensure his safety. Raul rolled his eyes with a small smile before departing the room.

"So," Hunter said as the door clicked closed, "what's the plan, sir?"

"We're going to get Ariana Monterro back and kill absolutely fucking everybody involved in her abduction," Jack said flatly. "Officially, as far as the United States government is concerned, we are most definitely not here to do anything other than consult and assist the locals in an advisory capacity only. Unofficially, the colonel is pulling every string he can to get us intel."

"And the locals?" Mostyn asked warily. "Monterro seems pretty friendly."

"He's put me in charge of the investigation and of recovering Miss Monterro. The Guàlizeans will see that we have any equipment we might need, and extra manpower too if required."

The three new arrivals glanced at each other, eyebrows rising, but they were all too well trained to question Jack's statement. "So we're sanctioned mercenaries for the duration, in effect, sir?" Hunter checked.

"Correct. Anyone got a problem with that, I'm sure you can figure out how to get back Stateside the same way you came."

Three shrugs answered him, and Jack smiled. He knew these men. Hunter might appear brash and cocky, but he was on the fast track to promotion, a superb officer even in the ranks of the Rangers, and Mostyn and Diaz were among the finest non-commissioned officers in the regiment. He could hardly believe that Lieutenant Colonel Cullane had sent him all three of them, but then, it was possible that Cullane had decided he could only send three men and asked for volunteers.

"In any case, I'm glad you're here," he said genuinely. "We don't have a target, yet, but I'm hoping that it won't be long. Monterro will see that we're well-armed, and there will be backup from the Guàlizean army if it comes down to it."

"Thought we were the backup, sir." Hunter gave him a mischievous grin. "We figured all we'd have to do was hold your coat."

The other man was irrepressible; despite his grief and worry, Jack found himself smiling back. “I hope so, Lieutenant. I truly hope so.”

Gutierrez found them rooms in a nearby hotel and dropped them off there to get a meal and some rest. Jack knew he wouldn’t sleep, but he also knew that he needed to try, because he had no idea when they might be called to action. Sitting down in the restaurant with the others, he looked at the menu unseeingly, unable to stop himself from wondering what Ariana was doing. Was she eating? Was The Black Wolf mistreating her?

“McAuley!”

A firm hand on his wrist jerked him back to the present, and he blinked, realizing Hunter was asking a question. “Sorry, I was somewhere else.”

“I could see that. What do you want?” Hunter gestured to the waiter, who stood by the table, pad in hand.

“Oh.” He hadn’t even really looked at the menu. “A steak, please. Medium rare, with a garden salad?”

Fortunately that seemed to be on the menu, because the waiter just nodded amiably and took his menu along with the others.

“Drinks?” the waiter checked, looking surprised when all four of them ordered water. With the possibility of a rescue operation needing to be mounted at any minute, none of them would take the risk of ingesting alcohol until it was all over.

“So,” Hunter said cheerfully once the waiter had brought their water and a basket of bread rolls, “tell us about your girl, Captain.”

Jack almost snorted the water he’d just sipped back out through his nose, glaring at the other man. Hunter grinned back, unabashed.

“That smart mouth is gonna get you in trouble one of these days, Lieutenant,” Jack growled finally, grabbing a bread roll. He could see the two sergeants grinning in his peripheral vision and decided not to take issue with their good-natured teasing. The presence of the three experienced Rangers, all of whom he knew well and could absolutely rely on, improved the chances of success in the mission to retrieve Ariana considerably. If, that is, they were able to find somewhere to retrieve her from. Morosely, he crumbled the bread roll between his fingers.

"Are we wrong, sir?" Hunter asked after a few moments of silence. "Is she not your girl?"

Sighing, Jack let the remains of the roll fall to his plate. "She isn't mine, no." He looked up to meet Hunter's eyes. "But if we don't get her back, I'm not sure there'll be much left for me to live for."

"Got it, sir," Hunter said with a nod, and Mostyn and Diaz both echoed the gesture. "We'll get her back, safe and well… and then you can work on convincing Ms. Monterro that she does want to be your girl."

"Quit while you're ahead, Hunter." Jack fixed him with a mock-menacing glare, which didn't repress Hunter's knowing grin in the slightest but at least quieted his teasing.

Their meals were delivered a short time later and the four men tucked in. Jack wasn't hungry, despite the excellent quality of the meal placed before him, but he forced himself to eat as much as he could get down. He was nudging the last bite of steak around his plate with his fork, wondering if he could choke it down, when the phone in his pocket vibrated. He almost ripped the fabric dragging it out, but the message on the screen read only, no news. get some rest.

Jack's jaw clenched. Shoving his plate away from him, he put the phone back in his pocket and answered Hunter's quizzical look with a curt shake of his head.

"Hurry up and wait," Hunter said, tilting his chair back on two legs. "Story of my life."

It was the story of any soldier's life. The waiting this time, though, would be worse than any Jack had ever endured, because his mind would not be silent, would not stop imagining what Ariana might be enduring at the hands of El Lobo Negro and his ruthless henchmen.

Jack knew the worst of what could happen. He'd seen it firsthand, and Ariana had too, six years before at their first meeting. He would never be able to forget the sight of Luisa Monterro's bloodied, battered body as he'd carried Ariana out of that place, doing his best to shield her from the sight.

Chapter Nine

Huddled on the bed, arms wrapped around her knees, trying to pull herself back from descending into the throes of a full-blown panic attack, Ariana couldn't help but have her mind drift back to the last time she'd been kidnapped. It was supposed to be a wonderful family holiday in Anguilla, a relaxing week away from the pressures of her father's new appointment to the justice ministry.

They had stayed at a private villa belonging to a friend, enjoying the beach and the warm limpid waters of the Caribbean. Raul had enjoyed a couple of fishing trips on his friend's luxury yacht, and it had been while he was away on one such afternoon trip when the peaceful idyll of the villa was shattered.

Guàlizean rebels, guerrilla fighters seeking to overthrow the government, invaded the villa and took Luisa and Ariana Monterro hostage.

Ariana remembered too much about that horrible afternoon. She had been certain that no help would be coming; Anguilla was a tourist paradise with little in the way of a police force, never mind paramilitary units with hostage rescue expertise. Some of the villa's staff had escaped and would be raising the alarm, but what good would that do? She listened in despair as the guerrillas' leader made phone calls to the Guàlizean President, demanding the release of convicted terrorists from jail, demands that would never be met no matter what the guerrillas did to their hostages.

Luisa had held her daughter tight, whispering in her ear that everything would be all right, when Ari knew very well that it wouldn't be. The hard, calculating eyes of the guerrillas as they watched her, their gloating smirks; the way their leader had run his eyes over her body had told her clearly that everything was most definitely not going to be all right.

She squeezed her eyes shut as the flashback hit. Her mother, standing up, pushing Ari back when one of the guerrillas had grabbed at Ariana's arm. Offering herself in her daughter's place, deliberately ripping her blouse open to show her still-lovely figure, telling the guerrillas that she wouldn't fight them as long as they left Ariana alone.

"No," Ari whispered, wishing she could deny what had happened. The fact that she'd been too frightened, too cowardly to move, as her mother let the men use her, one after another, Ariana huddling in the corner, eyes squeezed shut, wishing she could block out the grunts and gasps.

Until the gunfire started outside, the distinctive chatter of military-grade automatic weapons.

"The bitch has been delaying us deliberately!" one of the guerrillas shouted, and the first of a dozen knives pierced Luisa Monterro's flesh, her agonized screams echoing in her daughter's ears still, six years later.

Ari took a shaky breath. Pulled her hands down from her ears. No gunfire. No screams.

No bloodied, dead body of her mother, sightless brown eyes beseeching her. She was alone. And this time, Jack wasn't going to kick the door off its hinges and throw a flash-bang grenade into the room.

Blinded and deafened, Ari had come back to her senses being carried out of the building by a huge soldier. Instinctively, she'd begun to struggle weakly.

“It's all right,” the man said in a deep, gruff voice. “You're safe, Miss Monterro. Your father sent us.”

She'd squinted around to see that they were surrounded by a group of heavily armed soldiers in combat fatigues and sand-colored berets. “Who are you?” she croaked out.

“Lieutenant James McAuley, Fourth Battalion, Sixty-Seventh Army Rangers,” he responded evenly, glanced down at her and smiled. “But you can call me Jack. Lieutenant McAuley's a bit of a mouthful.”

Had it been a youthful crush, or a bit of hero-worship? Ari wondered now. Whatever, she'd clung to Jack even once she was returned to her grateful, grieving father by the Rangers, who had flown in by helicopter from where they had been conducting training exercises on nearby Puerto Rico when the Anguillan authorities made a desperate plea to the US government for help.

And Jack had stayed with her; strings pulled to have him temporarily relieved of his duty, he'd guarded Ari diligently, at her side every waking moment, sleeping she knew not when, because more than once when she woke screaming in the night he was there almost instantly; coming in and telling her in his gruff voice that she was safe, that he wouldn't let anyone hurt her, while she clung to him as though to a lifeline, her tears soaking his uniform fatigues.

Raul had begged Jack to leave the Rangers, head Ari's bodyguards permanently, and she was pretty sure he'd been considering it. He was near the end of his current enlistment, less than a year away as she recalled. But, of course, her actions the night of her mother's funeral had put paid to that.

She'd held up through the day solely for her father's sake. Raul looked worn down, exhausted with grief. She'd stood steady at his side, tears streaking her cheeks but her slim body unbowed, taking strength from Jack's quiet, solid presence at her back, in a civilian suit but still just as fearsome as in his full combat gear, his dark scowl warning off anyone who pressed too close.

And afterwards, after Mama had been laid to rest in the Monterro family burial vault, after Raul had been led away by the President, his own expression grief-stricken, Ari had stood alone and lost, swaying, until Jack's strong arm went around her.

“Come, Miss Monterro. I'll take you home.”

Home, where everything reminded her of Mama. Home, where all she wanted to do was cry and scream and rage at an unfair world, where women suffered and died for the wars of men. Somehow, her grief had turned to fury and she turned on Jack, beating her tiny fists against his broad chest and screaming incoherently, tears flooding down her cheeks. He'd shared one glance with her other guards and scooped her unceremoniously up over his shoulder, taking her to her private quarters as she kicked and screamed. Dumping her on the lounge, he stood over her, looking down at her.

“There. Now you can do what you like and you won't make a fool of yourself. I'll never tell, Ari. Scream all you like, hit me if you need to, take it out on me. I don't mind.”

His stoic acceptance broke something in her, something wild, and she leaped to her feet, standing on the couch to put herself on a level with him, finally able to look properly into his green eyes.

“What if what I want is this?” she asked, reaching out to grasp onto his broad shoulders before she leaned forward to kiss him.

Startled, Jack had pulled back. “Ari...” was all he got out, though, before she wrapped her arms tightly around his neck, her lips plastering to his again.

He hadn't resisted her after that, not when she started tugging at his tie, ripping at the buttons of his shirt, fighting to get him out of his clothes. His strong fingers had gently pressed hers aside before he removed the items that she wanted gone so desperately, showing her what she wanted to see, the thick muscles of his upper body, the strength of an elite combat soldier used to marching for days on end with a heavy pack of weapons and ammunition.

"You're sure?" he asked her one last time. Ari nodded, yanking at the zip of her dress, cursing under her breath as it stuck, until once again he took over, moving around behind her and easing the zipper down gently. Slowly, he pressed a kiss to her shoulder as he pulled her sleeves down her arms. Ariana's eyes fluttered shut as he unclasped her bra, hands sliding around in front of her to lightly cup her breasts.

Jack marveled at how soft Ariana's skin felt under his roughened, callused hands; her breasts were silken smooth apart from her nipples, hard little berries between his fingertips as he tweaked lightly, testing how sensitive she was, how hard she liked to be touched. Her soft moan told him that he was definitely on the right track, and he lost his head entirely when she whispered his name and trembled, her head falling back against his shoulder.

"Ari," he whispered huskily, letting his hands drop from her breasts, only to lift her up in his arms even as she whimpered a protest. Carrying her easily over to the bed, he laid her down on the silken sheets, gazing wonderingly down at her as she reached up to him.

"Come to me, Jack..."

He could have denied her nothing at that moment. Kneeling on the bed beside her, he reached to remove her shoes, slide his hands gently up her slender calves. She closed her eyes and smiled, lifting her hips so that he could more easily remove her dress, her panties, the garters holding up her sheer stockings.

“You are so beautiful...” delicate and fragile, she was the most perfect thing Jack had ever seen. Terrified of hurting her, he hesitated until she grabbed his hand and brought it back to her breasts with a whispered;

“Please, Jack.”

All thoughts of hesitation gone, he kicked off his shoes, lay down on the bed beside her and drew her into his arms. A tiny voice in the back of his mind pointed out how stupid he was being, but Jack had no intention of listening to his conscience just then. Not with Ariana warm and willing in his arms, her slender hands eagerly exploring his chest and shoulders, pleasured little sounds coming from her throat as he caressed her breasts. She arched into him; determined to pleasure her, he shifted down the bed, took one peaked nipple into his mouth, flicking his tongue over it teasingly for a few moments before closing his lips to suckle.

Ariana cried out, her fingers running over his close-cut hair, nails digging in lightly, letting him know that she wanted more, wanted him to keep going. One large hand skimmed gently down her stomach, parted the thatch of silky black curls at the apex of her thighs, teased lower. Her knees parted, hips lifting, and Jack groaned as his questing fingers found her already wet, her slick coating his fingers.

Her head fell back as he applied the tip of his index finger to her bud, rubbing in a swift, tight circle that sent her quickly spiraling upwards, her nails clawing at his shoulders. He kept licking and suckling at her breasts as that remorseless finger drove her on, stimulating her until she was crying out mindlessly, begging desperately for more, trying to pull him closer.

One long, slender leg hooked over his hip, Ariana tugging frantically at Jack. "Please, Jack, please," she sobbed, "I need you, please..."

At least he could be quite sure she wasn't mistaking him for someone else, Jack thought vaguely as he moved back a little.

"Easy," he soothed, "gonna give you what you want, my darlin'. But I'm not gonna rush this; you deserve more than that, deserve everything good I can give you."

"Please, I need…"

"I know what you need, my darlin'," he kissed slowly down her stomach, tasting her, tracing his tongue over her skin in teasing patterns. His hands wrapped around her knees as he shifted lower, lifting them over his shoulders to bracket his head. "Gonna give it to you, too," Jack whispered, nibbling lightly at the delicate crease where her inner thigh met her body before moving onwards to sweep his tongue slowly over her folds.

Ariana found herself drifting on a quiet haze of remembered pleasure as her mind disassociated from the unpleasant future awaiting her, taking her back to that long-ago night of bliss in Jack's arms. She was glad beyond measure that she had never told him the truth, that he was her first, because she was absolutely certain that he would have stopped. That he wouldn't have shown her what ecstasy could be found between lovers, what passion she was capable of.

Jack had been utterly unselfish, determined to bring her pleasure, and what pleasure it had been! His expert hands and mouth had brought her to the brink time and again before he finally let her fall; and when she did, he was waiting there to catch her in strong, steadying arms. Finally stripping off his suit pants, he'd found a condom in his wallet and used it, protecting her when she was far beyond caring anyway.

Impossibly aroused as he'd made her, she felt no pain when he eased gently, carefully into her, even though it was her first time. Encouraging her to wrap her legs around his hips to take him in deep, his strong hands held her hips steady as she writhed against him.

"Easy, my darlin'," he whispered again, sweat breaking out on his forehead, until he could hold out no more against the ecstasy threatening to overwhelm him too. "Ariana," it sounded almost like a prayer on his lips as he began to thrust, driving her back up again to that plane of ecstasy where everything floated away and there was nothing but the pleasure welling deep inside her body, the roughness of his chest hair chafing over her nipples, his hot skin sliding against hers, her name on his lips as he cried out and strained against her.

Perhaps a girl would always remember her first lover fondly, Ariana thought whimsically; but then Jack had been far more than that.

He'd been the one that got away.

Chapter Ten

Lying in the darkness, sleep seemed very far away for Jack. He lay wide-eyed, watching the reflections of headlights from cars passing on the street outside move across the ceiling.

After finishing their dinner, the four Rangers went to their hotel rooms, all aware that they should get as much rest as possible while they could. Professional soldiers, they were all well accustomed to catnapping, had long since learned to fall asleep at a moment's notice even in seriously uncomfortable positions.

So Jack couldn't understand why sleep eluded him now. He squeezed his eyes shut and counted sheep, did deep breathing exercises, and finally got out of bed and did a hundred push ups, as fast as he could.

Standing at the window afterward, watching the traffic pass by, Jack breathed slowly, feeling his pulse slow back to its usual steady pace. He tried to empty his mind, prepare himself to rest, but a niggling little thought kept squirming back to the forefront of his consciousness.

The last time I was in this city, I was with Ariana.

He'd never expected to visit Guàlize at all. Like most South American countries, Guàlize had a wary relationship with the US. The two countries' militaries had been involved in joint training exercises in the past, though never on Guàlizean soil, and while Guàlize had sent a contingent of troops to both Iraq and Afghanistan, and supported any number of UN operations, Jack couldn't say he'd ever worked directly with any of their troops.

When then-Captain Brody Cullane got a call from the higher-ups to tell him that his contingent of Rangers in the middle of a jungle training exercise on Puerto Rico was the closest potential response force to a major incident on Anguilla, Jack had been incredulous, but he'd jumped into the first helicopter like the professional soldier he was.

The last thing he'd expected to find in the villa they'd stormed was a terrified, traumatized girl sobbing over her mother's bloodied body. Ariana hadn't even realized how close to death she herself had come; Jack had put two bullets in the head of the guerrilla who'd been just about to stab his combat knife into Ariana's back.

She'd been stunned by the flash-bang grenade he'd tossed into the room to give them the element of surprise, her brown eyes wide, pupils unfocused, her ears almost certainly ringing with shock. He wasn't even sure if she could see him. Crouched on the floor as she was, he must have appeared a giant towering over her if she could, so he slung his gun around to his back and spread his hands, crouching down and trying to look as nonthreatening as possible.

"Miss Monterro?" He didn't even know if she spoke English, but his Spanish was high-school and poor enough that she might not understand him anyway. “My name’s Jack. I’m here to get you out.”

The tac chatter in his ear was telling him that the villa was now secured, so he took her arm to help her up, but she didn’t seem to be able to stand on her own. Hoping she wasn’t hurt, Jack lifted her into his arms, surprised when she relaxed against him and rested her head on his shoulder.

“I have Miss Monterro,” he said, heading for the door. “She’s secured. Medical assessment required.”

“Mrs Monterro?” Cullane asked.

“Negative,” Jack said crisply. “She’s a casualty.” He made sure to keep the girl’s face turned away from the sight of the bodies scattered in the hallway as he carried her out. She didn’t seem to notice the blood spattered up the walls from the head shots; he hoped she was still stunned from the flash-bang.

It wasn’t until he carried her outside into the villa’s shady courtyard where the team was regrouping that Ariana seemed to regain some awareness, beginning to struggle weakly in his arms. He reassured her gently, trying to keep his voice low and soft as he told her his name, and she surprised him by not only relaxing in his arms but reaching up to hook an arm around his neck and hold on tightly.

“Don’t let go, Jack,” she whispered in a voice thick with tears.

“I won’t,” he promised, and he’d held onto her until the medics arrived. They wanted to put her in an ambulance and take her straight to hospital, but she clung to Jack in a desperate panic.

“Don’t leave me!”

“I got you,” he reassured at a nod from Captain Cullane. “Lie down on the stretcher here and I’ll ride in the ambulance with you, okay?”

“Her father’s gonna meet you there,” Cullane advised over his radio as the ambulance pulled out. “I’ll arrange to have you rejoin us later. Stay with her; consider yourself her bodyguard until Monterro gets their own people on it.”

"Roger that, sir," Jack agreed before switching his radio off.

Ariana's grip on his hand was so tight his fingers were turning white. Reaching over, he pressed his free hand gently down on hers. "It's all right, Miss Monterro. I'm here."

She studied his face with wide brown eyes; what she saw must have reassured her, though he couldn't imagine how, streaked with jungle-colored greasepaint, sweat and gunpowder as he was. Maybe he just looked dangerous enough that she felt confident nobody else would attack her, but her grip loosened slightly.

The paramedic riding in the back of the ambulance with them leaned forward, asking in the thickly accented English of the islands if Ariana was hurt. She shook her head silently.

"You're sure?" Jack asked. He'd seen soldiers in deep shock die of wounds they didn't even realize they'd sustained; Ariana was most certainly in shock. The only blood he could see on her was on her hands, though, and he was pretty sure that was from her mother's body.

"They didn't touch me," she whispered; he had to strain to hear her over the ambulance's wailing siren. "Mama kept them off me."

"Okay." He ached for the pain behind those words, the way her face twisted up. "You've been very brave. Hang on now. We'll be at the hospital soon and your dad will be there."

She took his instruction literally, clinging to his fingers with that white-knuckled grip, even once they arrived at the hospital and she was rushed to a private area apparently reserved for VIPs. There were local police everywhere and they blanched at the sight of him in his combat gear, assault rifle still swinging on its strap behind him, sidearm on his hip and all sorts of other weapons clearly visible.

One of the police officers, more senior or perhaps just braver than the others, stepped forward to intercept Jack. "You can't go in there," he started, and Ariana screamed.

"No! No! Don't let go!" She jolted upright on the stretcher, grabbed at Jack with her free hand. "Don't leave me!"

“I’m not leaving,” Jack tried to keep his voice soothing even as he stared the police officer down. “You’re safe, Miss Monterro. I won’t leave you. I’m US Army Ranger Lieutenant McAuley,” he rattled off his serial number too, and the policeman finally nodded and backed down.

Raul Monterro was waiting with what Jack suspected was quite possibly the small hospital’s entire complement of doctors; the look on his face when he saw Ariana was terrible, a mixture of relief and anguish Jack hoped he never had to see again. He stepped forward to embrace his daughter, and she finally let go of Jack to throw herself into her father’s arms.

Perhaps he could have backed away, slipped quietly from the room and left her to her father’s care, but it never even occurred to Jack to do so. He’d made a promise and he intended to keep it.

And so, that night he found himself on a private jet heading to Guàlize City, on temporary leave from the Rangers until the Monterro family released him. Raul Monterro had been fervent in his thanks, and when Jack tried to brush it aside, saying that any Ranger could have been the one to find Ariana, Raul had looked him in the eye and thanked him for staying with her, as well.

In those first few days, Ari had panicked whenever Jack was out of her sight. The Guàlizeans Raul brought in to supplement her bodyguard had been wary of Jack, watching his every move, but his willingness to set everything else aside to care for Ariana finally won their respect. He'd slept on a cot outside her bedroom door, ready to leap up on a moment's notice if she made even the slightest sound.

Jack had never questioned his immediate devotion to Ariana. She needed him and so he was there. He talked to her, comforted her, did his best to distract her by teaching her card games, asked her about her hopes and dreams. She hoped to go to medical school in the United States and had endless questions for him; Jack only wished he had traveled more so he could answer her better. He'd grown up in Atlanta, gone to college at Georgia State on a football scholarship and joined the army on graduation after it became obvious he wasn't good enough to make football a paying career. Tough, athletic and smart, it wasn't long at all before he was encouraged to try out for the Rangers.

He'd visited more countries overseas on deployment than he had American states; that hadn't changed in the last six years. Still gazing down at the street, quiet now in the early hours of the morning, Jack scrubbed his hands through his short-clipped hair before sighing and turning back to the bed.

It did no good to dwell on the past. He needed to be well-rested and fresh in the morning, because extreme action was likely to be the immediate future.

Jack just hoped that Ariana was still alive to be rescued this time, too.

Chapter Eleven

Ariana was jerked from her reverie, her thoughts of a night six years past she'd never been able to forget, when the door once again opened without warning. She glared at Tomàs, who stared right back with an arrogant smirk on his lips.

"Dinner time, Ariana."

"Fuck off."

"I told El Lobo you'd say that. He instructed me to tell you that you can either put on one of the pretty dresses he chose for you, or that I am to cut everything you're wearing to rags and drag you downstairs naked. Either way you're going downstairs to dinner." Ostentatiously, he drew a sharp hunting knife from a sheath strapped around his thigh and began to clean his fingernails with it.

Fury choked Ariana to silence for a moment before she spat “Get out.”

Tomàs raised a mocking brow.

“Get out. He didn’t tell you to stay in here to make sure I changed. So get out. And don’t you goddamn well dare open that door again without knocking first and waiting for me to tell you that you may come in.”

For a moment, she thought she was about to lose the battle of wills, but clearly Tomàs was worried about what El Lobo might do if Ariana told him that Tomàs had refused her that civility. He dropped his gaze first and walked out of the room, the door thudding closed behind him.

Ariana took a deep, steadying breath before getting off the bed. One look in the closet confirmed her suspicions; El Lobo had no taste whatsoever. She flicked through the gaudy dresses with her lip curled up in distaste before finally selecting the least offensive and heading into the bathroom. She still had no plans to take a shower in there, but she was going to have to use the toilet and at least wash her face and hands. Doing so without giving any hidden cameras a view of any part of her body she didn't want seen was something of an exercise in contortionism, but she managed.

Changing into the ugly dress was somewhat more of a challenge, but in the end she decided to step into the closet. It was a pretty tight squeeze and dark, but at least she could be sure she wasn't giving Tomàs or Gustav or anyone else an eyeful.

Opening the bedroom door, she looked up at Tomàs. "So let's go."

"You haven't done your hair or makeup," Tomàs said critically, looking her up and down.

"He specified wearing one of his repulsively ugly dresses, not made up like a whore," she snapped back.

"And you haven't put any of the shoes on..."

"Because you gave him the wrong shoe size. I'm not going to break a goddamn ankle because you're too dense to know that all of mine are custom-made to fit my feet," she lied, rolling her eyes at him. She hadn't even tried on any of the ghastly spike-heeled stilettos. They might make a weapon in a pinch but there was no way she'd be able to move faster than a mincing walk in them, and Ariana had no intention of hobbling herself that way.

"Spoiled little rich bitch," she heard Tomàs mutter behind her as she strode ahead of him towards the stairs, ignoring the flouncy fabric swishing around her legs.

"I'm certainly accustomed to better than I'm receiving here, and I have every intention of pointing that out to Gustav," Ariana flung back over her shoulder, and had the pleasure of seeing Tomàs turn pale. Of course, it would have been his job to pass on not only her clothing and shoe sizes, but also her food preferences. She took a malicious delight in determining to pretend disgust in whatever she was served.

Not that she would need to pretend disgust, Ariana realized a few minutes later, wrinkling her nose in distaste. Tomàs had apparently indeed passed on her food preferences, all of them — and Gustav, in a stupidly extravagant attempt to impress her, had apparently ordered every single one of them prepared. There was enough food laid out on a long, polished mahogany dining table to feed an army, not just the two of them. The sight of so much food, most of which would undoubtedly go to waste, sickened her.

"You look lovely, Ariana," Gustav held a chair for her to sit. She stared at him for a moment before letting out a put-upon sigh and sitting down gracelessly.

"Champagne?" Gustav lifted the bottle for her to see.

"I don't drink. Didn't Tomàs tell you that?" Ariana said coldly.

Gustav cast a furious glare at Tomàs, who lifted his shoulders in an apologetic shrug.

"My apologies, sir, I didn't realize that it might be relevant."

Sitting down in his own chair, Gustav poured himself a large glass and took a healthy swig before asking "Why don't you drink, my dear?"

“I don’t drink, smoke, or do drugs,” she looked pointedly at the mirror lying on a side table she’d noticed as soon as she entered the room, lines of cocaine cut up on it, a discarded straw lying to the side. “I’ve just completed my medical degree; I’ve seen the damage all three can do.”

“You’re missing out. The pleasure rush brought by cocaine, it’s like no other.” Gustav grinned widely. He’d already indulged, Ariana realized. His pupils were dilated, his speech rapid, words tumbling over each other. She said nothing in response. There was no point.

“Water, Tomàs,” she pointed imperiously to some sealed bottles standing on the sideboard. Tomàs frowned at her, then jumped when Gustav surged to his feet.

“Why do you hesitate? Get it for her, immediately!”

Tomàs almost fell over his feet in his hurry to bring Ariana the water bottle. She took it from his hand with a regal nod, cracked the top and took a sip.

"What would you like to eat, Ariana? Please, these dishes have been prepared especially for you..."

She felt sick just thinking about it, about where the money had come from to pay for all this, about the sheer waste of it when so many people were suffering because of El Lobo's filthy trade. But she did need to eat, so she silently reached for a nearby dish of pabellón a criollo, the local delicacy of beef and beans on rice topped with fried egg, and scooped some onto her plate. At least she could eat it using just a fork in her one good hand.

Gustav wasn't eating — no surprise, she thought, knowing that cocaine usage depressed the appetite — and he continued to talk while she ate. He was acting almost manically, waving his arms expansively, telling her all about the money he had spent to build the house, the architect he had hired from Spain and flown here especially for the purpose. The background she had wondered about on seeing that he was white; his grandparents had left Germany in the 1940s, his father born in Argentina, his mother a Russian.

Ariana just ate in silence, listening. Gustav paused regularly, and she realized he was waiting for her to comment, but she honestly had nothing to say. Did he expect praise, for profiting from the blood and tears of her people? Joy, that he was the descendant of a man who had obviously been a Nazi hiding from justice? After the fourth time he paused and stared at her expectantly, getting only stony silence in return, she heard Tomàs snicker faintly behind her, from where he stood by the door.

"You dare laugh at El Lobo Negro!" Gustav leaped to his feet again, but this time he drew his gun, pointed it directly at Tomàs. "You have failed me!" he was shouting, spittle gathering at the corners of his mouth. "She does not drink my champagne, she does not wear the shoes I chose, she does not eat this food!"

"She is a rebellious brat who does not understand her true situation," Tomàs said, his voice steady and calm despite the gun pointed at him. “She will learn soon enough that it is in her best interests to please you.”

“Fuck you, asshole,” Ariana spat at him. “Two fucking years you’ve watched me and you still don’t know shit about who I really am.”

“I know you’re a spoiled little bitch!” Tomàs shouted back at her.

The crack of El Lobo’s gold-plated gun was thunderously loud, in the confined space. A red star bloomed suddenly on Tomàs’ forehead before his eyes glazed over and he collapsed like a puppet whose strings had been cut.

It was instinct that had Ariana leaping to her feet and racing to Tomàs’ side, but before she even knelt to check his pulse she knew it was too late. He was dead before he even hit the floor.

“You killed him,” she said numbly. She’d seen death during her training, of course she had; but seeing people die and watching someone be casually murdered in front of her were two very different things. “You killed him!”

“Your fault!” Gustav shouted back at her. “Look what you made me do!”

“I? I did not make you shoot him in the head, you monster!” Shocked and angry, she shouted back at him without even thinking about it. He pointed the gun at her face.

“Do not think that I will not shoot you, too!”

Kneeling beside Tomàs’ body, she should have cowered under the threat, but everything in her rebelled against doing so. Instead, she held Gustav’s eyes while her hand moved slowly, stealthily, toward the knife still sheathed on Tomàs’ thigh.

“Fucking bitch,” Gustav muttered before turning away, walking back towards the mirror with the lines of cocaine cut ready on it.

Now, Ariana thought. Nobody had come running to the room at the sound of gunfire, undoubtedly nobody would come running if they heard screams, either. She grabbed the knife in her unhurt left hand and leaped, fully intending to slit Gustav’s throat open with it.

He heard her coming as her shoes skidded on the polished marble floor; spun to face her with preternatural speed. The knife was in her left hand, though, not her right, and he had his gun on that side; he hesitated, just long enough for Ariana to kick him as hard as she could in the kneecap. Her left wrist swung up, no longer trying to stab but blocking the gun, pushing it up away from her face, silently cursing her near-useless right wrist.

The gun went off with an even more deafening crack this time, since it was so close to her face. Ariana blinked with shock. There was a brief, stunned silence as they stared at each other.

Gustav shoved, and Ariana was pushed back, unable to resist against his drug-fueled strength. The gun snapped down to point at her face again, and she froze, wondering if he would just shoot her.

Surely he must realize that I only have value as a hostage if I'm alive...

"Patrón?" There was a loud knocking at the door.

“Come in,” Gustav called after a moment, his jaw gritted.

Two men came hurrying in, having to shove Tomàs’ body aside to get in the door. They barely glanced at it, only looking at their boss.

“We heard a gunshot, patrón. Is everything all right?”

These men were a great deal more deferential than Tomàs had been, Ariana realized. That had been his fatal mistake, not acting with sufficient subservience to satisfy El Lobo. Gustav expected nothing short of devotion from his men, would tolerate no defiance.

Which might work to her advantage. If she could somehow take him out, there was probably no strong second in command; she might be able to convince the men to let her go. First, though, she needed to figure out a way to kill Gustav.

“Everything is fine,” Gustav said, though he did not take his eyes off Ariana. “Fuentes annoyed me.”

She refused to grieve for the traitor who had sold her to El Lobo, but that didn't stop shock at seeing him murdered in front of her eyes from taking its toll. Her hand began to shake, but she refused to lower the knife, would not back down even with a gun pointed at her face.

"Take her back to her room," Gustav said finally. "She needs some time to think on her situation and understand that it is in her best interests to co-operate."

Fat chance of that, Ariana thought, baring her teeth in a silent snarl. Both the sicarios eyed her, still wielding her knife, with caution. She gripped it tighter. Gustav snorted.

"What, are you cowards? Who are you more afraid of, her or me?" The gun in his hand swung towards the nearer man, and both men moved fast, coming in towards Ari in a pincer movement. She knew it was coming and moved too, hoping to take at least one of them out, but she took her eyes off Gustav to do it and his hand cracked down on her wrist. It was the hand wielding the gun and the heavy metal smacked down painfully on the delicate bones, making her scream with pain. The knife clattered from her hand and the two sicarios grabbed her arms, yanking her towards the door.

Ariana cursed and struggled all the way back to her room, tears of rage and pain pouring down her cheeks as both her aching wrists were painfully jarred. She had the nasty suspicion that the blow on her left wrist might have fractured her radius; it hurt even worse than the nagging ache from the sprained right one.

“Get in there, Monterro bitch!” She was shoved into her room, the door slammed behind her, and she heard the distinct click of a key turning in the lock.

Collapsing back to lean against the door, shaking with reaction, Ariana took deep breaths, fighting to stave off a panic attack. The night’s ordeal might not be over yet; Tomàs had implied earlier that El Lobo planned to bed her. There was probably little she could do to stop the drug lord if he came to rape her, especially with both her arms injured, but she might at least slow him down. Grabbing a couple of shoes from the closet, she jammed the pointed toes under the door as best she could, digging the spike heels hard into the carpet, before pushing and shoving a heavy, ornate chair over and wedging the top of it under the door handle.

Exhausted after the effort, her left wrist screaming with pain, she sat huddled on the carpet for a long time, her eyes on the door. She had no illusions that Gustav could not break it down, or order his men to do so, but at least she had done everything she could to protect herself.

Finally, thinking that she should try to get some rest and her precautions with the door would at least give her warning if anyone attempted to get in, she pushed herself slowly up and went to the bathroom. Tomàs had brought more than one bandage earlier and she could wrap her left arm, even if she was now quite sure that it was fractured. Probing gently around the purple lump swelling on her forearm brought tears to her eyes and made her suck in an agonized breath, but she couldn't feel any bones actually out of place. A stable, closed fracture, she tried to console herself. Not so bad.

“Pull yourself together,” Ariana told her reflection in the bathroom mirror. She looked terrible, pasty and sweating, not that she cared about how she looked at the moment, but going deep into shock might incapacitate her just when she needed to have her wits about her.

What would Elliot say?

“Triage,” she could almost hear his gruff, steady voice. “You know how to do that.”

Right. “Triage,” Ariana said aloud, and turned to look for the spare bandage she remembered Tomàs almost throwing at her. She’d put it on the dresser in the bedroom, she remembered now.

Bandaging her arm made her want to throw up, and with her right arm stiff and aching she couldn’t pull it anything like as tight as she needed, but she wasn’t about to knock on the door and ask for help. Showing weakness was literally asking for trouble.

Next step was to get out of this hideous dress. Thank God she’d chosen one without a zip, though the slippery fabric stymied her efforts to pull it off over her head.

"For fuck's sake," Ariana snarled finally, yanking at the neckline. The flimsy material parted easily, tearing straight down to her waist, and she finally fought free and threw it to the ground.

Only then did it occur to her to worry about cameras. Whatever, she thought, too tired to care. She still had her underwear on. There was a fluffy bathrobe hanging on the back of the bathroom door; pulling it on wearily, she found a washcloth lying beside the basin and wet it to wash her sweaty face.

Drinking unfiltered tap water wasn't the best idea, but it looked pretty clear when she ran it, and it wasn't like she had too many other options. Dehydration was a bigger threat right now, in her considered judgement, so she scooped a couple of handfuls and drank it down.

Finally, exhausted beyond measure, she half-staggered back into the bedroom, pushed the repulsive jaguar fur throw off the bed, and collapsed onto the silken sheets, careful despite her weariness to lay on her back and put both her injured arms across her stomach. With any luck, El Lobo wouldn't try anything during the night and she'd feel a little better by morning. Her eyes drifted closed and she fell quickly into a fitful, restless slumber.

Chapter Twelve

It was the sound of his phone ringing that woke Jack finally from a light sleep; he catapulted off the bed and grabbed it.

"McAuley," he snapped.

"Another email arrived, telling me where to collect a message from El Lobo Negro," Raul said succinctly.

"Don't you go and get it!"

"Go teach your grandmother to suck eggs, McAuley." Raul chuckled humorlessly. "Gutierrez would break my legs if I even thought about it. I've sent one of my men. He'll be back in an hour or so; I thought you'd probably want to be here."

"You're right, of course." Jack rubbed his free hand over his eyes, walking to the window to look out. It was still early, the city drowning in early morning haze, washing everything in shades of smoky gray. "Do you want me to bring the others in with me?"

"Best to keep you all in one place out of the public eye, I think. I'll have a car sent for you, and get breakfast brought in here. Thirty minutes," Raul added by way of farewell before hanging up.

The other Rangers had rooms on the same floor; a couple of quick raps on each door from Jack had them all quickly on the move, and by the time the car arrived for them they were showered, dressed and alert.

"With all due respect, sir, you look like shit," Hunter muttered quietly to Jack as they waited in a corner of the lobby. "Didn't get much sleep?"

"You have no respect at all, Hunter," Jack said in response, ignoring the question. "I'm ready to rock and roll. Don't worry over me."

"The only reason we're here is to worry over you, sir," Diaz, clearly eavesdropping on the conversation, put in. "When the colonel asked for volunteers, he nearly had a riot on his hands when he said he could only send three. Half the regiment wanted to come, but he said that would probably constitute an invasion and we'd better not."

"How'd I end up with you three idiots then?" Jack grumbled without heat, knowing that Brody Cullane could not have sent him three more competent soldiers. Hunter laughed at him, as a large black SUV pulled into the portico under the hotel.

"Guess you just got lucky, sir."

Shaking his head, Jack hid his smile as he climbed into the front seat of the SUV, the three Rangers chuckling as they got in behind him. A woman wearing the uniform of the Guàlizean Federal Police nodded to him from the driver's seat, her brown eyes calm and steady.

"Good morning, Captain," the woman said in lightly accented English. "I have instructions to take you to the Presidential Palace. These are for you and your men." She handed over laminated security badges.

"Thanks." Jack handed out the badges, took a moment to clip his own to his shirt pocket. He knew better than to ask the driver for any details of what had happened overnight. While he guessed the woman was probably one of Raul's own trusted bodyguards, keeping the information as closely held as possible was only wise when they had no idea who might potentially be on El Lobo's payroll.

It wasn't a long drive to the Presidential Palace. Jack hadn't really appreciated the beauty and grandeur of the building the day before, and he hadn't been there on his previous visit to Guàlize. He gazed now, impressed, as they drove down a long avenue lined with bougainvillea trees in full bloom, a riot of color which only served to highlight the stately beauty of the white marble palace.

"Is the whole government housed here?" Hunter asked from the rear seat. "It looks big enough!"

"Only the cabinet and the chambers of Congress," the driver advised. "Other politicians have their offices in the New Government Building, which is just behind the palace."

"Bloody impressive anyway," Hunter murmured, and Jack nodded in silent agreement.

They were all asked to show their passes at the security gate, while two more federal policemen went over the underside of the car with mirrors and an explosives-sniffing dog ranged around the car.

It was a sobering reminder that Guàlize was a country that considered itself to be in a civil war, with the current government taking a hardline stance against the drugs trade. Raul Monterro was not the first politician to pay a heavy price for his loyalty. Jack only hoped that he and his team could help stop El Lobo and make sure that Ariana did not become the latest casualty in Guàlize's fight against the narcos.

Raul was pacing his office when the Rangers were shown in. Gutierrez nodded to their driver, who had escorted them there, and the woman saluted before departing, closing the door firmly behind her.

"Is your man back yet?" Jack asked.

“He has arrived back at the palace, but the package he collected has to clear security before being brought in.” Raul grimaced and continued pacing.

“Because it would be a magnificent opportunity to deliver a parcel bomb or a contact poison directly into your hands,” Gutierrez said almost placidly. It was clearly an argument he had delivered before, and he was absolutely correct, Jack realized. El Lobo Negro had to have at least some suspicion that his kidnapping of Ariana would not provide his desired results. It had to be tempting to use the opportunity to take out Raul Monterro, the country’s Minister for Justice, a man who had dedicated his career to fighting the war on drugs and who had won some remarkable victories in the last few years. The cartels which had once virtually owned Guàlize, had elected members to high office and operated with complete impunity, were all but extinct.

While Jack was considering that, Gutierrez rose to his feet. “We’ve had food brought in,” he said, “there’s a dining room just through here.”

The other three Rangers followed eagerly, and Jack hesitated only briefly before going along too. He needed to keep his energy reserves up, and pacing alongside Raul would do nobody any good. It certainly wouldn't make the palace's obviously efficient and thorough security forces do their jobs any faster.

The room attached to Raul's office was obviously intended for the Minister to entertain small groups for meetings, but with its long mahogany table and antique upholstered chairs it made a very elegant dining room. A wide array of fruit, cold cuts, cheese and several types of bread tempted the Rangers to sit down and tuck in, though as Jack filled his plate he couldn't help wondering what Ariana was eating, indeed if she was being fed at all.

Ariana woke with a start, hearing a sound in her room. She'd left the lamp beside the bed switched on, not wanting to wake up in complete darkness, and in the faint light could see the door handle turning, someone trying to open the door from the outside.

It was very dark outside. She silently cursed her habit of going without a watch — she'd stopped wearing one during med school when she found that she was forever getting surgical gloves caught on it, but it would have come in handy right now, because she had no idea what time it was.

The handle twisted again, the door shaking. Frightened, Ariana grabbed for the closest thing to a weapon she'd been able to identify in the room, one of the spikiest heels from the closet. Hissing with pain as her injured wrists protested, she still scrambled out of bed and moved to stand beside the door, waiting. If whoever was outside managed to get it open, she fully intended to try nailing them in the eye with a stiletto heel as they entered.

Standing this close to the door, she could pick up the low-voiced conversation outside it.

"Come on, get it open," one voice exhorted.

"I'm trying! It's jammed somehow."

"Bitch must have wedged it shut from inside. We'd have to break it down."

There was a brief pause.

"No, it'll make too much noise. El patrón will kill us if he catches us. Leave it. She'll still be here tomorrow night. We can wait."

Coarse laughter reached Ariana's ears as they moved away. She took a deep breath and sagged against the wall. She had absolutely no doubt that she'd just escaped a violent rape by the skin of her teeth, and quite likely had only delayed it for a few hours.

"I hope you've got a plan, Papi," she whispered, fighting back welling tears. "And I really hope it's a good one."

Creeping back to the bed, she huddled under the covers even though the room was warm, clutching the spike-heeled shoe close until morning finally came.

The Rangers had finished eating and were drinking coffee, though there was no chatter in the room as they waited for Raul's man to arrive with the package from El Lobo. Finally, a knock on the door of the outer office had them all jumping to their feet.

Gutierrez rolled his eyes, waving them back and wagging a finger under Raul's nose when he headed for the door himself. Jack smiled as Raul backed off, looking chastened; Gutierrez was obviously a top-notch bodyguard. He certainly had his principal well under control.

The package was brought in by a nondescript Guàlizean man with the steady eyes of an experienced operative. He evinced no surprise at finding his boss's office full of American soldiers in civilian dress, just scanned them all over with those steady eyes before handing a small plastic carton about the size of a shoebox to Gutierrez.

"The original packaging has been sent off for fingerprinting and DNA test," he said in rapid Spanish, "along with a few strands of the hair, to check that it is indeed Señorita Monterro's."

Gutierrez nodded, placing the carton carefully on the desk. Removing the lid, he frowned as he and Raul peered into the box. "Was there a letter?"

"No." The newcomer shook his head. "No letter. It was a cardboard box wrapped in brown paper, Minister Monterro's name written on the outside. I was there when Security opened it; the only thing inside the box was a plastic bag with that in it."

Raul reached into the carton and removed the contents; Jack saw now that it was a hank of hair, about ten inches in length, tied at each end with a piece of cheap brown twine. Something deep inside him recoiled that something so coarse should touch even a severed piece of Ariana's hair. She deserved nothing less than the finest of silk ribbons. The cheap twine was just another insult.

Jack listened in silence as Gutierrez grilled the other agent on the details of the pickup, but there was really nothing to tell. They'd received an email just after dawn telling them to make the pickup at a small park in a distant part of the city; the agent had found the box underneath a park bench, picked it up and come straight back. Nobody else was even in sight.

“Thank you,” Gutierrez said at last, clapping the other man on the shoulder. “Good job today.”

A calm duck of the head as the agent with the steady gaze accepted his due, and then he was gone, the door closing quietly behind him.

Raul had sunk to sit down in his hair, running the length of Ariana’s hair between his fingers, his eyes closed. He looked like a man in terrible pain.

There was silence in the room for a long, awful moment, and then, behind Jack, Sergeant Diaz spoke quietly.

“Why wasn’t there a letter with the hair, sir? I thought the original email said it would be delivered with a list of demands?”

“No doubt that’s coming in another email,” Jack said, catching Gutierrez’s eye. The Guàlizean nodded, reaching to open the laptop and typing quickly. “A letter, whether hand-written or typed, is just another piece of evidence, after all."

"There's a new email," Gutierrez said grimly. "Arrived a couple of minutes ago."

"Read it," Raul said wearily, not bothering to open his eyes. "Tell me what he wants, that I shall no doubt have to refuse. Tell me what the price of Ariana's life would be." He sounded resigned, exhausted. Jack got the strong impression Raul had a pretty good idea already what El Lobo Negro was going to ask for.

"I take it that by now you have received the token your daughter sent for you," Gutierrez read from the computer, first in Spanish and then translating into English for the Rangers' benefit, although all of them were at least moderately fluent in Spanish. "To purchase her another day with all her body parts still attached, you have until midnight tonight to arrange the release from Santa Luisa Prison of Juan Gabriel Alvarez."

Raul laughed bitterly. "Alvarez. Of course. That son of a bitch."

“And who is Alvarez?” Jack asked, though he reckoned he could take a pretty good guess.

“Assassin, enforcer, call him what you will. We knew he was involved in El Lobo’s organization when he was picked up some three weeks ago in a stop at the Colombian border,” Raul said, finally opening his eyes. “It seems that he may be of more importance than we realized. Give the order to have him moved to solitary confinement and questioned again, Ramón. Clearly, he knows more than he’s told us.”

“He’s told us nothing, sir!”

“Exactly.” Raul’s expression was merciless. “If Ariana must pay the price, so will Alvarez. Squeeze him.”

The Rangers exchanged glances. Nobody spoke as Gutierrez blew out his cheeks, but said nothing in response to Raul’s order. Instead, he took a phone from his pocket, dialed a number and walked into the adjoining room, speaking in rapid Spanish to whoever answered on the other end.

Jack watched Raul for a minute or two, and finally said “Do you mind if I forward the email to Lieutenant-Colonel Cullane, sir? I sent the first one on for the NSA to maybe run a back trace."

Staring into space, Raul waved a negligent hand. "Do what you wish with it."

Jack heard feet shifting behind him, looked over his shoulder to see Hunter giving him a concerned look. He shook his head minutely, letting his lieutenant know that he wasn't worried. Yes, Raul was acting a little oddly, but he was just coming to terms with new information. The brilliant mind that had made Raul Monterro the finest prosecutor in Guàlize before he was tapped to join the ministry of justice would soon start ticking over again.

By the time Jack had forwarded the email on to Brody Cullane with a request for an update on any tracing efforts on the previous email, Raul had opened his desk drawer and taken out a small velvet box. Placing it on the desk, he opened it before putting the hank of Ariana's hair down on the polished timber beside the box.

Jack watched as Raul's neatly manicured nails made short work of picking free the knots in the coarse twine, before he placed the scraps in an ashtray he took from the same desk drawer. He took his time carefully coiling Ariana's hair into the velvet box, wrapping it around something that gleamed gold on the dark velvet.

"My wife's wedding ring," Raul said without looking up from his self-appointed task. Finally, he closed the box and placed it back in his desk drawer, closing the drawer silently. "Does anyone have a light?" he asked, lifting his head at last.

Jack considered pointing out that the string was also evidence, but he kept his mouth shut as Diaz fished in his pocket to produce a lighter and offered it up.

"Thank you, Sergeant," Raul said courteously, and flicked the lighter. They all watched silently as the string burned to black ash, a faint acrid scent rising briefly before the air conditioning swept it away.

The scrape of Raul's chair was loud in the quiet room as he pushed it back. "Well, gentlemen," he said, and his voice was sharp and clear again. "Let's be about it."

Gutierrez came back in from the other room, snapping his phone closed. He paused to sniff at the air, eyes narrowing, and then shook his head as he saw the wisps of smoke curling up from the ashtray.

"Try not to set fire to any more evidence, sir?" he requested dryly.

"El Lobo does not care what evidence we find," Raul replied with a shake of his head. "The whole point of this is that he is finally coming out into the open, brazen and defiant. Why would he care if we find his DNA in traces of saliva on an envelope?"

"Because then we would know who the bastard actually is!" Gutierrez's face twisted in a snarl, and Jack realized that the steady, professional bodyguard was a lot more emotionally affected by the situation than he'd shown so far. "We would know his name, his prior associates, the people he cares about!"

There was a low growl of agreement, and Jack was a little surprised to realize that it had come from his own throat.

“Easy, skipper,” Hunter said quietly behind him.

Raul was watching him, Jack saw, and the expression on the older man’s face was not unhappy in the slightest. After a moment, Jack gave Raul a nod, and received one in return.

Yes, Jack would do whatever it took to get Ariana back.

Whatever it took.

Chapter Thirteen

The sun had well and truly risen, and Ariana had well and truly lost her temper. The balcony doors which had been open when she woke up the previous afternoon had been locked at some point when she was out of the room meeting El Lobo, and the room quickly became far too warm. There was an air conditioning unit on the wall, but no controller in the room, and the fan on the ceiling didn't respond to any of the switches.

She'd expected someone to open the door and give her some breakfast. Nobody came, though, and when she grew impatient with the rumbling of her stomach and rapped a shoe against the door, loudly demanding attention, there was no answer.

Putting her ear to the door, Ariana listened. She knew it wasn't soundproof, from the conversation she'd heard the previous night, but she could hear absolutely nothing.

Leaving the door and going to the balcony doors, she peered out, squinting against the bright sunlight. She'd seen trees outside yesterday, but taken little notice. Now she looked properly, and saw not just trees, but the high triple canopy of the deep rainforest. There was a cleared area around the house, though, and peering through the window and between the wrought-iron bars of the balcony she could see lush, flowered gardens. Pressing her cheek against the glass to peer left and right, she saw another building beyond one end of the house, but couldn't quite discern its function. A garage, perhaps?

There wasn't a single soul in sight. Gritting her teeth with frustration, she debated putting her shoulder to the balcony door and trying to smash it open, but then what? Even if she made some sort of rope out of her bedsheets, her injured wrists would prevent her from climbing down to the ground. And if she were somehow able to get to the ground, she had no idea where she was; the very presence of the high-canopy rainforest told her she wasn't in Guàlize City, or any other town. That meant escape on foot was out of the question. She'd be lost in the jungle within minutes.

She would need some sort of vehicle to make an escape attempt with any chance of success, and that meant stealing one. Squinting again at the building that might possibly be a garage, she wondered if they left the keys in the ignitions. If they were in an isolated area, they might well be casual about such things; why worry about theft if there was nobody about to steal?

With a sigh of frustration, Ariana went back into the bathroom and ran some cool water over her wrists, splashed her hot face. At least she had water to drink, and it hadn't made her sick the previous night, so she had to assume it was safe.

Damn El Lobo to hell. He'd figured out how dangerous she was, realized he couldn't let her talk to his men. Perhaps she'd overplayed her hand with Tomàs.

On the other hand, it had given her potentially valuable information; El Lobo was quick to lose his temper, liked to indulge in his own product, and trusted nobody.

Now if only she could figure out how to turn that against him somehow.

Returning to the bedroom, Ariana lay down on the bed, her brain spinning with possibilities and plans. Because Ariana Monterro might be going to die out here in the jungle, but she most certainly wasn't going down without a fight.

The day seemed to last an interminable number of hours. The President himself stopped by Raul's office to ask if there was any news, an expression of grave concern on his face, promising Raul any resources he might need.

"The news is very tightly held," he promised Raul. "Nobody has asked me anything; I have not heard Ariana's name so much as whispered."

"Yet," Raul said darkly. They all knew it was only a matter of time; El Lobo was very likely to call the TV stations himself once he concluded that Alvarez wasn't being released from prison.

Raul had several meetings scheduled in his office with officials from the Ministry that morning, and after some heated discussions he eventually decided that he should not cancel the appointments, to keep up the illusion of normality as long as possible. The Rangers would go into the adjoining room to wait until the meetings were over.

Gutierrez provided a pack of cards and assured them that the room was soundproof, and the team fell back on the time-honored tradition of soldiers waiting for action, playing endless hands of cards. Jack couldn't concentrate, though, on edge every time the door opened.

More food was delivered at lunchtime, cornmeal arepa cakes filled with ham and cheese and tajadas, deep fried slices of ripe plantain. Hunter eyed the jug of dark brown liquid with ice cubes floating in it that accompanied the food with suspicion.

“That doesn’t look like iced tea.”

“Tamarind juice,” Jack told him. He remembered it well from his previous visit. It had been a favorite drink of Ariana’s, and though it was an acquired taste, he’d come to enjoy it too.

Why can I not forget a single thing about her?

He knew why even as he asked himself the question. Ariana Monterro was unforgettable, even at nineteen; what she might be like as a woman of twenty-five almost terrified him.

Raul was picking at his food, Jack saw, Gutierrez watching him closely with a concerned expression on his face. When the phone on Raul’s desk rang, Raul was first to his feet, almost running into his office.

Jack caught Gutierrez’ eyes. “He’s right on the edge,” he advised, concerned.

“What can I do?” the agent said quietly, with a resigned shrug. “Until this is over, nothing can be normal.”

“Ramón!” Raul slammed down the phone, came barreling back into the room, his eyes alight with fervor. “Alvarez is talking!”

Gutierrez was on his feet at once. “You want to go there, to question him.” It was a simple statement of fact.

“Of course.” Raul turned to Jack. “We cannot take you with us, though. American soldiers in the Presidential Palace is not so strange; for me to take even one of you into Santa Luisa Prison would be something else entirely.”

“I understand,” Jack said, and he did. He wanted to be there himself, to squeeze the details of Ariana’s location from the drug runner, but he had to trust in Raul’s men to get the job done.

“I’ll get my man to take you back to your hotel. Get some rest; if we get the details from Alvarez you could be moving out in a few hours,” Gutierrez advised.

Frustrated, Jack balled his fists under the table, but he nodded. There really wasn't anything else he could do.

Ariana woke with a start, unsure at first what had woken her, until the rumble of a diesel engine reached her ears. The room was a little cooler, but she still felt hot and sticky. Pushing herself off the bed, she hurried to the balcony doors, peered out just in time to see a jeep coming out of the jungle on a rough track that led around the back of the building behind the house. At this distance, she could not make out any detail, could not discern more than that the jeep carried a driver and one passenger.

Maybe now they'd actually feed her. Her room faced east, so the sun was behind the house now, but from the shadows she could tell that it was late afternoon, probably after four o'clock.

With the jeep's arrival, the compound suddenly seemed to come to life. Had El Lobo been away, and his men slacked off, lazing about in his absence?

Perhaps she'd never know for sure whether or not her hunch was correct, but within ten minutes after the arrival of the jeep, there were footsteps outside her bedroom door. Wary, Ariana watched the door from where she stood beside the window, startled when it opened to reveal not sicarios, but a plump middle-aged woman carrying a tray.

"Who are you?" Ariana asked in surprise.

"I'm Emilia, miss," the woman replied placidly, setting a tray down on the side table. There was a bottle of water on it and a plate with some slices of cut-up fruit. Starving hungry, Ariana couldn't keep her mouth from watering as she looked at the plate. "El Patrón thought you would prefer me to look after you, rather than men you don't know," Emilia continued. "Is there anything you need?"

It was a dumb question, Ariana thought. "A gun and a getaway car?" she suggested sarcastically.

Emilia didn't look remotely surprised. "You will be dining with El Patrón at seven," she said with no inflection in her voice. "Wear a nice dress." Turning on her heel, she left the room, the door clicking shut behind her followed immediately by the sound of the key turning in the lock.

At least the water Emilia had brought was cold, and so was the fruit. Ariana ate everything on the plate and drank all of the water. The air conditioning had come back on, and her room was finally cooling down. Sitting on the end of the bed contemplating her options as she sipped the last of the cool water, she thought glumly that she should have asked Emilia for some books to read, because just one day shut in her room with nothing to do and she was already going stir-crazy.

Heading to the bathroom to wash the sticky fruit juice from her hands, it occurred to her that there was at least one thing she could do, even if it would provide her with only a momentary satisfaction. She could go over the bathroom inch by inch and find any cameras, figure out a way to block them so she could take a shower without worrying about some pervert watching her. Her trick of blocking the door had worked pretty well last night, so she went back into the bedroom to repeat it, jamming a heel under the door and wedging the ornate chair under the door handle again.

It didn't take her long to find the first camera on top of the mirrored wall cabinet, pointing directly at the shower. A firm yank and the wire came out of the wall, making her smile with satisfaction even though her wrist twinged painfully. She didn't stop looking, though, and she soon found a second camera, this one rather better concealed in a natural knot in the wooden paneling on the walls. She considered how to deal with that one for a minute, head cocked to one side, before smiling again. A squirt of toothpaste in the lens should take care of that, and at least El Lobo was apparently concerned enough for her dental health that he'd provided toothbrush and toothpaste.

Ariana searched for ten more minutes, but she didn't find anything else. In the end she took a deep breath and shrugged fatalistically. If her kidnappers saw her taking a shower, even if they made a tape of it and uploaded it to the internet, realistically at the moment that was the least of her potential worries.

Unwinding the bandages around her wrists hurt, but she needed to look at them, and she knew only too well that they weren't tight enough anyway. Once she'd washed, she would try and tighten them up. When nobody had come bursting in — or attempted to — by the time she'd finished removing the bandages, she decided it was time to risk the shower.

The hot water felt wonderful against her sweaty, grimy skin. Ariana turned her face up to the spray and let it wash away her troubles, just for a few seconds. The steady background throb of her aching arms pulled her back to reality sooner than she would have liked, and she sighed and reached for the soap to wash herself quickly and get out of the shower before anyone intruded on her.

Washing her hair had been a nightmare with both arms hurting and drying it was out of the question. It was just going to have to be a tangled, damp mass. Maybe if Emilia returned, Ariana could ask for her assistance to comb it out and braid it, but she wasn't going to knock on the door and ask for the other woman.

Sighing, she contemplated the contents of the closet. The one halfway-reasonable dress she'd worn last night was now nothing more than torn rags. Of the dozen or so dresses remaining, she couldn't imagine ever wearing any of them. The short dresses were so short her ass would barely be covered in them, and whatever the skirt length they all had plunging, immodest necklines. Her bra would be more than half visible under any of them, and she certainly wasn't going to leave it off.

Eventually she shrugged and grabbed a dress made of some stretchy, silky material. It was patterned in garish colors which would hopefully draw the eye rather than her half-exposed bra, and at least the stretchy fabric meant she didn't have to struggle with zips. Wriggling into the dress, she grimaced at her reflection in the mirror.

"It'll have to do," she muttered, turning away from her reflection. She wasn't about to struggle with any makeup, and if El Lobo said anything about it, she'd use her sore wrists as an excuse. She would never paint her face and pretend to be his whore, no matter what he threatened or did to her.

Chapter Fourteen

The female agent with the steady eyes was the one who met the Rangers in the parking garage, another black SUV waiting for them. She didn't offer her name, and they didn't ask it as she drove them back to their hotel.

"I'm gonna go have a shower and see if I can catch a few hours shut-eye," Jack said quietly as the four men paused briefly in the hotel lobby. "If you want to go out to have a look around, that's okay, but keep your phones on hand." Gutierrez had supplied them all with cheap pay-as-you-go mobiles, never previously used, to keep in touch.

"Stay within five blocks?" Hunter suggested, and Jack nodded. The center of Guàlize City wasn't all that much bigger than that, and if they stayed within that area they could be back at the hotel within ten minutes if they had to move out quickly. Having come in on a commercial flight, none of them had any weapons to pick up anyway.

“Stay together if you do go out,” Jack requested. “The three of you, or at least two of you. We can’t know if we’re being watched, and I don’t want to offer up any easy targets.”

“Sir.” All three acknowledged the order with crisp nods. They’d have saluted had they been in uniform, Jack reflected as he turned for the elevator alone and the others headed back out the doors. They were presumably feeling a bit stir-crazy after the long flight yesterday and being cooped up all day today, needed to stretch their legs. As least he’d been out in the jungle yesterday, at the crash site. Thinking of that, he remembered that he needed to call Mara. He’d do it once he got back to his room. Raul had arranged for Elliot’s body to be brought back to Guàlize City with the others; because of the criminal nature of the crash, it was a legal requirement that they be autopsied. Elliot’s body would be released within a few days and Raul had promised to arrange repatriation for all the dead security detail.

It wasn't an easy conversation, sitting on the edge of his hotel bed in a darkened room, telling Mara that Elliot was definitely dead. That Jack had seen his body.

"There has to be an autopsy, but I should be able to bring him home in a few days," Jack told a crying Mara down the phone.

"An autopsy, why?" she hiccuped out. "He was killed in a plane crash!"

Belatedly, Jack realized he'd let the cat out of the bag. He should have just told Mara that there was red tape to deal with before he could repatriate Elliot's body, he thought, disgusted with himself. He wasn't about to lie to Mara, though, so instead, he said "Mara... there's more to it than I can tell you right now. Classified information."

She'd been married to a Ranger; she knew there were some things that couldn't be talked about. No doubt her mind would be racing with speculation, but she wouldn't say a word to anyone until he could give her more information.

"Ariana?" Mara's one-word question carried a wealth of meaning.

"Classified," Jack gave her a single word in response.

"I see." Mara went quiet for a moment before saying "Good luck, Jack."

"Thanks, Mara. I'll bring Elliot home as soon as I can."

"Thank you," she told him before saying goodbye and hanging up.

Jack lay back on the bed still fully clothed, gazing at the ceiling. In all the intensity of the hunt for Ariana and her kidnappers, he hadn't really had much time to think about Elliot's death. It still hadn't hit home that his best friend was really gone. Probably wouldn't until he was back Stateside, he mused, until Elliot could have the proper send-off he deserved. Just the thought that he would never see Elliot again, never hear the deep chuckle that heralded one of Elliot's terrible jokes, was too hard to comprehend just now.

He was tired enough after his poor night's sleep that when he closed his eyes, sleep wasn't too far away. He slept lightly, though, troubled by dreams of a faceless man hacking off Ariana's lustrous hair with a machete, lock by lock, getting ever closer to her scalp.

Jack startled awake from his restless doze at a loud rap on his door. To his surprise, he saw the light was fading outside; he'd slept for longer than he realized.

"Who's there?" he called, sitting up and swinging his legs off the bed.

"Hunter."

"Be right there."

The smaller man was alone when Jack opened the door. "Diaz and Mostyn are just washing up," Hunter said without preamble, "and then we're planning to go down and get some dinner. You coming?"

"I guess." Jack nodded. "Do you have a look around?"

"Yeah, we did. This is a beautiful city, huh? Not really what I expected from South America."

Waving Hunter into the room, Jack took a clean shirt from his pack and changed into it. "What did you expect?"

"I'm not too sure, honestly," Hunter shrugged. "Considering I've never been down here before... I guess I thought it would be all like the slums of Rio I've seen on TV."

Jack chuckled at that, picking up his jacket and shrugging into it. "Not in Guàlize, or not on any large scale, anyway. The country is sitting on a good-sized oil reserve on the north side of Lake Maracaibo, and they've had two honest and popular Presidents in a row, for the last fourteen years. They poured a ton of oil revenue into infrastructure and education, and your average citizen here is doing quite nicely, thanks very much. It's why Monterro and the rest of the government are so determined not to let drug cartels get a foothold here again."

"I get that," Hunter nodded. "There's a small market a couple of blocks from here, locals selling fresh produce and spices, that kind of thing. We chatted to a few of the stall owners and damn, they were nice people. Friendly when they found out we were Americans, too."

That was uncommon enough to warrant curiosity, Jack knew. He nodded as they left the room and headed along the hallway to knock on the others' doors. "It was like that when I was here six years ago, too. They're real friendly."

"Yeah, good people."

Mostyn and Diaz were ready to go, so the four headed down to the restaurant again. There were plenty of businessmen there in small groups, so nobody gave the four men a second glance as they settled down at a quiet table to the side of the room.

The same waiter who'd attended them the previous night returned to take their orders. Jack still found himself struggling to pay attention to the menu, so he just waited for Hunter to place his order and then said "Same for me, thanks."

They were halfway through eating their meals, talking quietly about the sights the men had seen that day, when movement near the door caught Jack's eye.

"Gutierrez is here." And from the look on the man's face, he had news. Jack dropped his fork on the plate and rose to his feet as Gutierrez approached the table.

"McAuley. We've found them," Gutierrez got direct to the point.

"Let's go. Oh, the meal," Jack turned back towards the table. "Better get the check."

"It's taken care of," Gutierrez waved off his concern. "Come. Mr Monterro is waiting for you."

They weren't heading back to the Presidential Palace, it immediately became clear as Gutierrez turned the SUV he was driving in a different direction.

"The airport," he said succinctly when Jack asked where they were headed, and with that, Jack had to be content.

"Is this wise, sir?" Hunter said in an undertone as the four Rangers followed Gutierrez out of the SUV and into a plane hangar. "This isn't military..." on the contrary, the plane occupying the hangar was an executive private jet, a gleaming new Gulfstream twin to the one Jack had seen crashed in the jungle.

“Can’t risk involving the Guàlizean military,” Jack said quietly back. “Not if we want the advantage of surprise. El Lobo Negro has eyes and ears everywhere.” He shared Hunter’s concerns, but he trusted that Raul Monterro wanted to give them the best possible chance of retrieving Ariana alive. He wouldn’t do anything to jeopardize that.

They appeared to be quite alone in the hangar apart from Gutierrez, who closed the door they’d entered by before heading over to the plane and calling up to the cockpit. A moment later Raul Monterro popped his head out of the open door, nodded when he saw them and came down the stairs.

“Just doing pre-flight checks,” he said as Jack gave him an inquiring look.

“I didn’t know you were a pilot, sir,” Jack said, a little surprised.

“A hobby,” Raul shrugged. “Fortunately, I am qualified to fly one of these jets. This one belongs to a friend who was amenable to lending it to me on short notice."

"To go where?"

"Come," Raul beckoned, and the Rangers followed him to a grouping of tables set up at the side of the hangar. Maps and photographs were spread out there, some of the ones that Jack had seen earlier and others new to him.

"What does your Colonel Cullane prefer to drink?" Raul asked unexpectedly.

"Uh... I'm not sure. Scotch, I think?" Jack said, caught off guard.

"I shall make sure to send him a case of the very best. He called back not long after you left; your NSA finally came through on tracing back the original email and my people were able to do the rest. The original signal was sent from this property here." Raul picked up a photograph and handed it over.

"Elaborate," Jack observed, studying the picture of the white ranch-style house. Three stories high and twelve full-sized windows across the front, it was a massive property which wouldn't have looked out of place in the Hamptons.

"And not something that just anyone can afford to build in Guàlize, you understand. Ostensibly, the property was built as an eco-tourism lodge. Trying to make a booking through their website — a website that is extremely difficult to find in the first place, and attempts to install viruses on your computer once you do — is all but impossible. The anti-narcotics department have had their eyes on the property for a while now."

"You think the property belongs to El Lobo Negro?"

"Indeed." Raul added some satellite photos to the image Jack held. "Not quite as good as those provided by the NSA, but Google are faster. Construction on the property was completed a little over a year ago and these images are four months old."

The images indeed weren't as high-resolution as the picture which had revealed the existence of the secret drug-runners road the previous day, but they were perfectly adequate for Jack's purposes. He spread them out on the table and he and the other Rangers pored over them, examining the buildings shown in the compound — there were several small ones in addition to the huge ranch house — and debating their purpose, and the possible numbers of hostiles they might find on site.

“We’re gonna need to go in well-armed,” Hunter said, tracing his fingertip over the buildings. “And we can’t drop right on top of the site. Need to come in and scout around.”

“No time for covert surveillance,” Jack said tightly. “We need to go in hot and take Miss Monterro out of there.”

None of them liked it, but they also knew he was correct. Jack saw the sideways glance exchanged between the two sergeants, though, and knew what they were thinking.

“We’re going to need some pretty serious firepower,” it was Mostyn who voiced it.

Raul cracked a smile. “Fortunately, I have thought of that.”

He gestured them to follow him around the plane to the other side of the hangar, where they stopped short at the sight of the weapons Gutierrez was busily loading with ammunition.

“I thought you said we weren’t getting army backup?” Hunter said.

“You’re not.” Gutierrez glanced at him, cracked a grin. “I’ve only got four parachutes.”

“And enough guns for half a regiment! Where the hell did you get all of this lot?” Hunter stepped forward, picked up a brand-new assault rifle and examined it, impressed.

“Don’t ask, don’t tell.” Gutierrez’s grin changed to a smirk.

There was fresh clothing for each of them as well, jungle-pattern camouflage fatigues, two full sets each, a pack already prepped with emergency medical supplies, and more ammunition and explosives than they could ever hope to carry.

They took fifteen minutes to make their selections and pack their gear before returning to the planning table. They might be rushing their entry, but Jack wanted to make damn sure they had multiple alternative extraction plans if things went south, because there was a high probability of something happening to screw up their basic plan.

Raul was impatient to get going, but Gutierrez was clearly ex-Special Forces and convinced his boss to be patient while the Rangers worked through their process. And it was a good thing that they didn't leave straightaway, because just as they finally wrapped up and prepared to load the jet, the sound of a car pulling up outside made them all freeze and look at each other.

Gutierrez was the first to move, drawing his sidearm and moving to the entry door. A minute later he turned to look at Jack, eyebrows raising, before bringing the newcomer into the hangar.

"You've got a visitor, Captain McAuley."

"Do I know you?" Jack asked in surprise; the local-looking man wasn't in the least familiar.

"Well, we only met briefly yesterday, and I didn't exactly introduce myself," the man said with a grin, and Jack suddenly realized he was the American agent who'd given him the satellite photographs in the park the previous day. "I don't know what you're doing here and I absolutely don't want to know — plausible deniability and all that — but I've got this for you. Just came in on the afternoon flight, in the diplomatic bag."

Jack's eyebrows flew up as he opened the bag the agent handed over, and a smile spread over his face. Inside were half a dozen of the Rangers' encrypted personnel radios. He'd hated the idea of going in without comms, but they couldn't guarantee anything they got in Guàlize would be secure. Having radios they were confident the enemy couldn't pick up on definitely boosted their chances of success.

"Good luck, Captain McAuley," the agent said quietly, before turning to address Raul respectfully. "I wish you every success in the speedy recovery of Miss Monterro, sir."

"Thank you," Raul inclined his head in return, and they watched as Gutierrez escorted the agent out again.

"Did we ever get his name?" Raul said after a moment.

“Do you really think he’d have given you his real one?” Hunter asked dryly in return.

Chapter Fifteen

Ariana had no way to know the time, but she assumed it was seven o'clock, or just before, when her door was unlocked again. She'd pulled the chair and shoes away to let the door open freely and was sitting by the window with her hands folded demurely in her lap.

It wasn't Emilia who opened the door; it was one of Gustav's sicarios, a thin man with a bushy mustache and the cold eyes of a snake. Another man stood behind him, round-faced and leering as he gazed at Ariana's cleavage. She ignored both of them, rising to her feet and walking past them with her head held high, serene and silent. Behind her, one of them murmured something she didn't quite catch, but the dirty laugh which followed it made the hairs stand up on the back of her neck.

Willing herself to keep her pace steady, Ariana descended the stairs. She had no intention of allowing a pair of thugs to intimidate her, not when the real threat awaited her in the dining room, smiling warmly and offering her a choice of non-alcoholic beverages.

"Water will be fine, thank you," she said coolly. "I don't particularly care for sugary sodas, and the aspartame in diet sodas is a terrible chemical. Carcinogenic."

Gustav actually ground his teeth, and Ariana wondered if he had made a special trip to get the sodas. Was he really making an effort to please her? Surely he didn't think she could be seduced by his efforts!

Ignoring him, she sat down at the table and looked at the food spread before her. At least there wasn't a feast fit for twenty tonight; there were only half a dozen dishes on the table, none of them grandiose or complicated.

Gustav poured a glass of water for her, and innate good manners made her murmur a quiet thank you. He took his own seat.

"Tonight we will know just how highly your father values your skin," he said maliciously.

"He does not value it above our country, I assure you," Ariana said in a bored tone, considering what she would like to eat. While the plate of fruit earlier had taken the edge off her hunger, she needed to keep her strength up even if she wasn't getting any exercise. She selected some quesadillas and placed two on her plate.

Gustav didn't seem to have indulged in the cocaine tonight, because he was eating, filling his plate and wolfing the food down with healthy slugs of red wine from his glass. His table manners were repulsive; Ariana did her best to keep her eyes on her own plate so she didn't have to see his open-mouthed chewing, the greasy fingers he wiped on his clothes.

The drug lord didn't seem to know what to say to her when he wasn't making threats. He made a few remarks that Ariana could almost have construed as flirting, if the compliments weren't so backhanded. Clearly El Lobo thought that women were the inferior sex, and treating them as though they might be intelligent beings with thoughts and opinions of their own was a foreign concept to him.

Ariana ignored her unwanted dinner companion as much as she could. Eating her quesadillas and drinking her water, she finished and sat silently with her hands in her lap.

"Why don't you talk?" Gustav said finally, apparently irritated by her attitude. "Women, they never shut up normally."

"Then my choice not to talk should come as a pleasant surprise," Ariana rejoined.

Obviously unable to find a counter to her logic, he stared hard at her. She could feel the weight of his gaze, but willed herself not to look up, just kept her eyes on her empty plate.

The silence was broken again, this time by the distinctive chatter of automatic weapons fire, and Gustav started to his feet, shouting for his men and drawing his gold-plated gun from inside his jacket. Ariana sat very still, not wanting to provoke him as the muzzle of the gun swung in her direction.

"We are under attack, patrón!" one of the men who had rushed into the room at Gustav's shout babbled, his eyes wide and frightened. It was the cold-eyed man who had opened Ariana's door earlier, and he didn't look nearly as confident now, she noted with restrained pleasure. "They are Americans!"

"Don't be ridiculous," Gustav snapped back. "Why would Americans be here? No, it's Monterro's men. Well, we shall see how willing he is to continue when his precious daughter's life is on the line. Take her upstairs and restrain her."

"Wait, what?" Ariana started to her feet, and cursed as the cold-eyed man grabbed her upper arm roughly. "Get your damn hands off me!" She looked at Gustav, but he ignored her, hurrying from the room, shouting for more of his men.

The cold-eyed man and his oafish partner from earlier half-dragged Ariana upstairs, muttering threats as she kicked and fought them.

"We'll deal with you later," the cold-eyed man told her with a leer, dragging her into her room. "It will be a pleasure to send your father a video of his precious daughter being used by every man who wants her." He followed the remark with a rough slap at her ass, and she shrieked with fury and fear, struggling to get away. Neither man had any intention of letting her go, though, and the situation rapidly got worse as one of the men produced a thick cable tie and secured her tightly to the bedpost, hands in front of her.

She could do nothing but scream her rage at the empty room after that, though thankfully the two men immediately left her alone. One jerk at the cable tie had her seeing stars, the pain in her wrists more than she could bear. Standing still, trying to catch her breath, she leaned her forehead against the wooden post and prayed that the next person in through the door would be coming to save and not kill or rape her.

The lights went out suddenly, and Ariana caught her breath. Alone in the dark, listening to the gunfire outside, she suddenly felt more afraid than she had through the whole ordeal. One way or another, her fate was about to be decided, and she had no say in it at all.

Chapter Sixteen

Sitting in the co-pilot's seat, Jack gazed unseeingly at the dark jungle below them as Raul piloted the plane expertly towards their drop point. Ariana was down there, somewhere, in the power of the man — the monster — he'd read far too much about in Raul's files that morning. The things El Lobo Negro had done, had ordered done, turned his stomach. The thought of what that bastard might do to Ari made Jack want to fall to his knees and pray.

"Ten minutes," Raul said quietly, and Jack nodded, getting to his feet. He placed a hand lightly on Raul's shoulder.

"We'll get her back." Or die trying, hung unspoken in the air.

“I know.” Raul took his eyes off his instruments, glanced up at Jack. Their eyes met and they shared a silent moment of communion, in the knowledge that this could very well be the last time they ever met. “Take care, Jack,” Raul said at last, and Jack nodded.

“You too, Raul,” he said quietly, hoping that he’d see the older man again before too long.

Heading back into the cabin, he nodded to the other three; Hunter nodded back. They already had their parachutes and gear on, ready to jump. Jack shrugged into his and clipped the straps, moved to the rear door and put his hand on the handle, awaiting Raul’s signal.

“Good luck down there,” Gutierrez said from the seat by the door. “Bring Miss Monterro home, Captain.”

The red light above the door blinked on. Jack grasped the handle and yanked up, opening the door; the air pressure drop sucked at him, trying to drag him out, but he held onto the frame firmly. He would go last. Hunter was the point man; he moved quickly past Jack and jumped into the howling darkness.

It took less than twenty seconds for all four Rangers to vanish into the howling blackness of the night. Gutierrez yanked the door shut and secured it before unfastening his straps and heading forward to take the co-pilot's seat beside his boss.

"Do you think they can pull it off, sir?" he had to ask.

"If they can't, then God have mercy on Ariana, because the Black Wolf will not," Raul replied. His voice was steady and his face might have been carved from stone for all the expression he showed, but Gutierrez could see how much he was hurting.

Silently, the bodyguard faced forward, looking out into the night. Under his breath, he whispered a prayer for the four men who'd voluntarily jumped out into the darkness to try and find Ariana Monterro just because one of them cared about her.

Plummeting into the darkness in free fall, time seemed to slow down for Jack, every second stretching into an eternity in which he could look back on the decisions he'd made which led him to this point.

It all began, he thought, the night after Luisa Monterro's funeral, when Ari had broken down and turned to him in her grief.

God forgive him, Jack thought grimly, but he'd been weak. Ari was beautiful enough to make any man look twice, and she could not have been more perfectly his type if she'd been made to order. She had thick dark brown hair all silky waves to the small of her back, lighter tawny-brown eyes sparking fire at him, her face a perfect oval of golden skin and full soft lips. As for her body, she was utterly delectable, slender curves and long limbs, pressed close against him as she clung to him and kissed him, offering herself up to him.

Inexcusably, he'd lost his mind. He'd been fantasizing privately about Ariana since he first met her; even though he kept telling himself it was wrong, somehow he couldn't stop. He'd never let it color any of their interactions, had never had any intention of letting her know how attractive he found her.

Until now, when she was wrapped around him, holding on tight, tugging at his clothes and making little sounds of frustration as she couldn't get them off quickly enough to suit her needs.

He kissed her back fiercely, ripping off his shirt and tie impatiently, letting her run her fingers over his thickly muscled chest. Her black dress had followed his clothes to the floor, the black silk bra, panties, garters and stockings beneath inflaming him to the point of madness.

He'd whispered her name against her smooth golden skin before tracing every inch of her with his tongue, because if he was going to do this Jack McAuley was damn well going to do it right. No rough, hasty coupling for Ariana. She deserved more, deserved tenderness, and he gave it to her, though there was little tenderness left in him by the time he rose over her and she dug her nails into his back, begging him for more, harder.

Tucking her sated and sleeping into bed and leaving her was the hardest thing he'd ever had to do, but he knew he'd already breached the one cardinal rule of bodyguarding.

Don't get involved with the principal.

He hadn't told Raul everything — he'd have been lucky to get out of Guàlize alive if he had — but he'd admitted that he believed he'd grown too close to Ari to be the impartial, clear-headed bodyguard she needed, and that he felt she in turn had grown too dependent on him, in her grief.

Raul, still red-eyed from his own grief, studied Jack for an uncomfortably long moment before nodding. "Fair enough, Lieutenant. Captain Cullane has provided me with a list of names to contact, Rangers who have recently left the service or are about to. Yours was first on it, but I wonder if you would take a look at the others?"

Jack could hardly refuse, so he sat down and looked at the list.

Elliot's name had been the second one on it, right below his own.

Jack closed his eyes with guilt for a brief second. If he'd accepted the job, if he'd somehow been able to refuse what Ari had begged him to take, would Elliot still be alive? Would Mara now not be a grieving widow? Would Ari be safely at Raul's side? God, what a mess. And now he'd dragged Hunter, Diaz and Mostyn into what would very likely be an absolute clusterfuck of a situation, one which it was very possible none of them would escape alive.

All because of a slip of a girl who'd held his heart in her slender hand for six long years, even though he hadn't laid eyes on her since that night.

The clock in his head ticked down to zero and he looked at his altimeter; the number glowed bright, telling him it was time to open his parachute. A quick flick of his wrist sent his pilot chute out, and the hard jerk against his chest a couple of seconds later told him that the main 'chute had deployed correctly.

Through his night-vision goggles, he could just make out the faint shapes of the other parachutes ahead of him, the men dangling below them a brighter green. They'd picked a hilltop about a mile from the compound for their drop zone; it was closer in than Jack liked, but a mile in the jungle was comparable to ten miles on open ground. It would take time to cross, even for men as experienced in navigating such terrain as the four Rangers. They had no intel on the situation they'd be facing, no recon but a few satellite photos, no idea how many men El Lobo might have on the ground.

They'd be lucky if any of them ever saw another dawn.

Jack's feet hit the ground with a dull thump; he absorbed the shock of the landing with the ease of long practice, quickly got to work removing his parachute and bundling it up. Diaz came up to take it from him and conceal it with the others; Jack nodded to the sergeant and reached up to switch on his radio. How Colonel Cullane had managed to get the encrypted devices into the diplomatic bag for delivery on such short notice Jack had no idea, but he'd be forever grateful, because there was no chance of The Black Wolf or his men intercepting their signals.

"Alpha Leader," he said crisply.

"Alpha One," Hunter responded instantly, and "Alpha Two", "Alpha Three" from Mostyn and Diaz came in a couple of seconds later.

"Alpha One, report."

"LZ is clear," came the crisp response.

In under five minutes, the hilltop was abandoned again, the four men moving through the jungle together, weapons at the ready. They rotated point duty between them, using a machete to cut through the thickest parts of the jungle where they had to, but relying on their night-vision goggles and Hunter's skills in particular to get them through more easily. Jack shook his head in some awe as Hunter once again found them a pathway though an apparently impenetrable thicket. The lieutenant had grown up in the thickly forested mountains of northern Idaho and it showed; even among the highly skilled and trained Rangers, Hunter was the best man 'in the woods' Jack had ever known.

"Did I mention before how very glad I am that you're with me?" Jack said quietly, directly into Hunter's ear, when they paused for a brief rest about halfway to their destination.

"You didn't, but thanks," Hunter replied, his voice amused.

"I mean it. The fact that the three of you volunteered to come down here…" he choked up, surprising himself.

"Don't sweat it, Cap," Hunter tapped him on the shoulder lightly. "This is what we do. Kill the bad guys, rescue the girl. Miss Monterro hasn't got a sister, has she?"

"If she does I call dibs," Diaz squatted down next to them, lifting his canteen for a drink, grinning, teeth gleaming white in his greasepaint-smeared face.

"She wouldn't go for your ugly mug," Hunter jibed.

Jack found himself smiling at the hissed insults they began trading, however briefly. Despite the fact that Hunter was an officer and Diaz an NCO, the camaraderie and trust between his men was something Jack had worked hard to foster.

He only wished that they had the rest of his company to back the four of them up. Another hundred and forty-odd men would come in damned handy right about now. Even a squad or two.

Jack spared another moment or two on the wistful daydream before nudging Diaz gently. “Knock it off.”

The two fell silent instantly. Jack touched his radio. “Alpha Lead, Alpha Two, report.” Mostyn had gone on a short distance to scout.

There was silence for a few seconds before “Alpha Two. Contact made.”

All three Rangers were on their feet at once. “Alpha Lead, Alpha Two, report!”

“Contact down. Proceed.”

“What the fuck, Mostyn!” Jack hissed as they made their way through the trees, came across the hulking sergeant bending over a prone body.

"The guy damn near pissed on me. He came into the trees to take a leak. I was just scoping the land."

They were speaking in hushed tones, relying on the jungle's background noise to keep their cover intact. Mostyn gestured ahead and Jack realized they'd reached the edge of a large cleared area. Lights not too far ahead must be the house itself.

"Couldn't take getting piss on you, Mostyn?" Diaz jibed.

"Didn't see the point. His life expectancy was under five minutes anyway."

The foot soldier was very dead, his head flopping loose on his neck. He wouldn't have had time to make so much as a squeak before Mostyn rose up out of the darkness and killed him.

"Did he have a radio on him? A dog with him?"

"Nothing. I don't think he was even patrolling, not properly. Just came over here to take a leak." Mostyn shrugged. "Sheer dumb luck that he picked the spot right where I was lying."

They all knew how a mission could go FUBAR in an instant from nothing more than bad luck. Jack counted his blessings, that Mostyn had been quick enough to stop the foot soldier from raising any alarm.

“No time for any more recon,” he made a snap decision, “just in case he’s missed before we’re in position. We’re going in. Right now.”

Chapter Seventeen

The Rangers had made a rough plan back in the hangar, which pretty much boiled down to kill everyone in sight and get into the house as fast as possible. The dead guard just meant they had to execute the plan a little sooner, without taking time to scout around first. Jack insisted on taking point, which all three of the others agreed was a terrible idea, but since he was their superior officer they couldn't talk him out of it.

Hunter made the decision that he was going to stick to Jack like glue to try and keep him alive, and directed Mostyn and Diaz to form a second team, to approach the house from the other side. They ran swiftly through the darkness, keeping their radio chatter to a minimum.

“Alpha Lead, Alpha Three; I have a guard barracks, ten hostiles inside.”

“Take it out, Alpha Three,” Jack ordered without missing a beat, and ten seconds later there was a loud explosion on the other side of the house. Jack grinned and saw Hunter’s answering grin as his teeth flashed white in the darkness. Diaz had a way with explosives and had loaded up with a gleeful grin on his face from the bounty Gutierrez had provided them with. Not that he’d have needed much; a grenade or two lobbed through the window would have done the job perfectly.

There was shouting inside the house and the front door swung open, three men rushing out and looking around frantically, guns in their hands pointing at the sky.

“Fucking amateurs,” Hunter spat beside Jack. The lieutenant was carrying a Mk 46 machine gun. Jack had rolled his eyes and commented about overkill when Hunter selected it, but he had to concede Hunter might have a point about its usefulness when one pull of the trigger took out all three of the sicarios.

There was shouting inside the house now, another explosion around the back, and all the lights suddenly went out.

“Found the generator,” Diaz said laconically over the radio.

“We gotta get in there,” Jack said, “they’re panicking. Look,” he pointed at the corner of the house. “I’m gonna climb that, go in a window. Cover me.”

“You fucking maniac!” Hunter hissed back at him, but Jack was already up and running at top speed. Gunfire from windows of the house peppered at his heels. Cursing, Hunter returned fire, spraying bullets at the hostiles, and the gunfire died down.

“Fucking hell,” Hunter said aloud, and then into the radio “Alpha One, Alpha Lead has gone in.”

“Fuck,” Mostyn said eloquently before he and Diaz both acknowledged properly.

“Alpha One, I’m gonna assault the front door,” Hunter said, hardly able to believe the words that were coming out of his own mouth, but he needed to create a diversion for Jack, give his captain a fighting chance at finding the hostage. “I’m going in.”

“Alpha Two, going in, there’s a door on the western side,” came the response a second later.

“Alpha Three, fuck it, I’m going in the windows.” There was a BOOM as Diaz blew something else up and Hunter winced before starting to run, his machine gun up and laying down a field of suppressing fire as he charged the front door.

The trellis Jack had spotted wasn’t really designed to carry a man’s weight, and certainly not someone as large and heavy as he was, loaded up with a full pack of weapons and gear. It creaked ominously as he hauled himself rapidly up, trying not to put his weight on any part of it for more than a fraction of a second. Coming up level with a second-story window, he swung out and went through it boots-first, dropping and rolling as he hit the floor, his rifle snapping up instantly, ready to fire.

The room was empty, he swiftly assessed through his night-vision goggles. He could hear heavy fire downstairs now as the other three Rangers stormed the house; running for the door, he found it locked.

“Fuck!” He didn’t waste ammunition shooting the lock, just leaned back and kicked the door off its hinges with a tremendous blow from his boot. A man passing in the corridor outside spun with a startled yell and Jack shot him right between the eyes.

“Kill her, kill the bitch!” a voice shouted tinnily in Spanish, and Jack’s face twisted as he saw the radio at the dead man’s belt. Stooping to grab it and the pistol beside it, he began to run along the corridor in the direction the man had been headed, throwing open doors as he went to glance quickly into each room.

“Is she dead? Tell me she’s dead, I want Monterro to find her corpse!” the voice screamed again, just as Jack threw open the last door to find Ariana, her face pale as she twisted to look at him, her hands bound to the bedpost.

Ariana screamed as the door swung open to reveal a man standing there. She couldn't see his face in the darkness; there were flames leaping outside but there were no lights on in the house and she could only see enough to make out that he was huge, bigger than any of the sicarios she'd seen here yet, and lifting a pistol in her direction.

She screamed as loudly as she could, quite certain she was facing her own death in the next few seconds and not about to go out in silence. The pistol went off with a deafening crack and she waited for the pain, realized that he hadn't hit her and stopped screaming in disbelief. He was less than four feet away. How could he possibly have missed at that distance?

"It's done, boss. She's dead," Jack said gruffly in Spanish into the radio, dropped it on the floor and crossed to Ari in one long stride, putting his hand over her mouth. “Don’t scream again,” he said, speaking in English this time, “if they think you’re dead it might buy us a minute or two.”

Bug-eyed with shock, Ariana watched as he set the pistol on the bed, drew a knife and slashed through the cable tie binding her to the bedpost. The huge man was American, and there was something very familiar about him.

“Who are you?” she asked.

“Captain McAuley, US Army Rangers, ma’am, you may remember me...”

Peering up into his face as he released her hands, she said in astonished wonder; “Jack?”

Jack startled as she said his name, looked at her face. He could see her a lot better than she could him, with his NVGs on; see her wide, startled eyes and parted lips.

“Yeah,” he said gruffly, “I’m here to get you out.”

Ariana couldn’t believe it. Jack, here. He’d come for her. Again. “Why?” she asked without even thinking about it.

"For your father, Ari! And for Elliot." Spotting the white bandage on her right wrist, Jack reached for it. "You're hurt?"

"Sprained. The other one's badly bruised, maybe fractured; my hands aren't much good for anything right now."

"Hopefully it won't matter. Come on. Do you think you can use a gun if you have to?" he picked the pistol up off the bed and offered it to her. While he was confident in his ability to protect her, leaving Ariana defenseless when he knew Elliot would have trained her to take care of herself would be a foolish move.

"I'll shoot that bastard El Lobo if I see him," Ariana muttered, taking the gun. The weight of it dragged at her aching wrists but she didn't care, using both hands to hold it pointed safely at the floor as she followed Jack towards the door.

He didn't have to tell her to stay close. She was no soldier but she knew what to do, had clearly been drilled thoroughly in how close to stay to the leader during an exfiltration. At least she was wearing sensible flat shoes, and though the tight silky dress she had on wasn't the most practical outfit he hardly had time to stop for her to change. He had to wonder what the hell had been happening before the Rangers arrived, but there was no time to talk about it now.

"Alpha Lead, I have the package," he said crisply into his com. "Meet at exfil point."

The gunfire elsewhere in the house was dying down now; the other three Rangers quickly acknowledged and Jack put out a hand to steady Ari as boots came clattering up the stairs towards them and she raised her pistol.

"He's with me. Don't shoot."

It was Mostyn; the sergeant nodded to Jack, casting a quick glance over Ariana. "Medic?" he asked Jack brusquely, obviously also spotting her bandaged wrists.

"Nothing critical."

At that instant, a loud clattering sound above their heads made them all look up.

"What is that?" Ariana asked.

Jack cursed. "The chopper!"

Mostyn whirled without a word, ran back to the stairs and sprinted up to the top floor.

"Go!" Jack hissed, and Ariana hurried after the other soldier, leaving Jack to bring up the rear. They got to the roof just in time to see the helicopter lifting off.

Jack didn't waste time on curses. He could already hear Hunter doing that on the radio, in between occasional bouts of gunfire. "Alpha Lead, Alpha Three: alternate exfiltration required," he said instead.

"All Alphas, Alpha Three, south-west corner," Diaz's voice came back a few seconds later.

The three of them ran for the corner of the roof, Mostyn shucking his pack and yanking a coiled rope and grappling hook out of it. There was nothing to be seen at the southwest corner yet, but Jack didn't doubt Diaz.

"Go, go!" he yelled at Mostyn, who nodded, slammed the hook into the roof and leaped off, abseiling down the side of the house in a forward sprint which made Ariana feel queasy just watching.

“I can’t…” she held up her hands to Jack. She doubted she could even get a decent grip on the rope right now, and she wasn’t wearing gloves.

“I know,” he said, slinging his rifle around to his back, taking the pistol from her hand and slipping it into a side pocket of his pack. “Put your arms around my neck.” He grabbed up the rope, braced his feet on the edge of the roof. “Come on, Ari. You know I won’t let any harm come to you.”

Two explosions went off simultaneously, not far away, bright orange flames lighting up the night, showing her his face properly at last. He was smeared in black and green jungle camouflage cream, still wearing those futuristic, alien goggles which covered his eyes.

How can you be so sure? she wanted to scream at him. It was a long way down to the ground, and they still had no visible escape route.

Jack just stood still, waiting. He couldn't make the abseil with one hand, not carrying his pack and Ariana. Much though he wanted to, he couldn't just grab her and take her to safety. She had to trust in him.

It didn't take her long. A couple of seconds and her quick brain came to the conclusion that she didn't have a choice. Two swift steps forward and she was reaching up to put her arms around his neck.

"I don't know how much grip I've got," she warned as he stepped back off the edge of the roof.

"Legs around me," he ordered.

He was thick with muscle and the pack and gear on his back made it very difficult, but as soon as he started walking quickly backwards down the side of the building Ariana felt instantly quite safe. He was so steady in his pace, his breathing loud but not labored in her ear as she clung to him like a monkey.

Amazingly soon, they were on the ground and Jack's arm went around her, steadying her, setting her on her feet and holding on until she was stable. He pressed her gently back against the wall of the house and turned to place himself between her and any possible danger.

Feeling suddenly very cold now she wasn't clinging to his warmth, Ariana hugged her aching arms around herself, wondering what was going to happen next. The other Ranger seemed to have disappeared, Jack was barking orders into his com, and she could still hear explosions and gunfire at what seemed to be a horribly close range. Every instinct was yelling at her to put her hands over her ears, squeeze her eyes shut and curl up into a ball.

Ariana felt her breathing coming faster, her heart beginning to pound in her chest. Her skin prickled. Not now, not now, I can't have a panic attack now! she thought frantically at herself. Pretend it's a training exercise, one of the many Elliot made me run through... the thought of Elliot made things worse, though. Elliot had been her rock for so long, knowing that he was gone and she'd never be able to turn to him for advice again only ratcheted her panic higher.

Fixing her eyes on Jack's broad back in front of her, she started silently listing all the bones of the human body to herself instead, starting at the feet and working her way up. She'd only reached tibia, fibula, patella, when there was a sudden roar of a vehicle engine and an open-topped jeep came rocketing around the corner of the house, screeching to a stop directly in front of them.

Jack whirled around, lifted Ariana off her feet, and literally leaped into the back of the jeep carrying her, taking her down to the floor and covering her with his body.

"We don't have Hunter!" he yelled at Diaz, who was driving. Mostyn beside him was standing on the passenger seat, rifle braced on top of the windscreen.

"Picking him up at the front door!" Diaz shouted back. The jeep was already moving again, lurching as Diaz ran over some carefully-tended flowerbeds before again skidding to a stop.

Hunter leaped agilely into the back, stepping on Jack's leg before seeing him. "Sorry, sir!" he yelled, crouching down beside him and turning to face the rear, bracing his machine gun on the jeep's tailgate.

Jack didn't even bother to respond. Through his NVGs he could see that Ari was lying quite still beneath him. Her lips were moving, though he couldn't hear anything.

Is she praying? he wondered. Well, a few words in the Almighty's ear certainly won't go amiss about now!

The jeep was bucketing forward again, the engine squealing with protest as Diaz mashed the gas pedal to the floor and pushed the vehicle to its limits. Hunter and Mostyn fired again and again, but the firefight only lasted a few seconds before suddenly they were away from the house and speeding along a dark jungle track.

Hunter tapped on Jack's back to let him know all was clear. Jack pushed himself up and twisted to sit down on the Jeep's floor. Trying to take one of the seats on the side would be a recipe for disaster at the speeds they were traveling on the rough tracks, so he just braced his back against the rear of the driver's compartment and pulled Ari up beside him.

She jolted hard, unprotected as he was by the pack on his back, so he lifted her over his thighs to sit in the vee of his legs with her back against his chest. He could speak to her more easily this way, his mouth right by her ear.

That was what he told himself, anyway, though he saw Hunter look back at him and grin. Jack studiously ignored his second's expression.

"Alpha Lead, all Alphas, any casualties?" he checked first.

All his men denied any injuries. Jack wasn't really surprised, despite the number of sicarios they'd faced. Armed, equipped and trained as superbly as they were, the Rangers would have had to be unlucky to take casualties against such opposition, not with the advantage of surprise. El Lobo and his men had been utterly outclassed.

Ariana, therefore, was his only concern at the moment. It was hard for him to tell, with the jeep's bumpy and erratic motion, but he was pretty sure she was shaking. She's in shock, he thought, and tried to wrap himself around her, to warm her.

"Ari," he said loudly in her ear. "Ari, can you hear me?"

She nodded jerkily against his chest.

"I'm gonna get you out of this. Your father's waiting for you. We hoped to take the helicopter, but we have an alternate plan."

Or course he had a backup plan, Ariana thought. Jack's steady, confident air helped her to feel more stable. Her shaking slowed, then stopped altogether. Subconsciously, she pressed closer against him, turned her head to rest her cheek against his chest.

Chapter Eighteen

Jack could only silently curse that he couldn't just stay here holding Ariana like this forever, her soft breath ghosting against his neck. For a few brief moments the noise of the jeep, the rough, jolting motions, everything faded away and his world narrowed down to the woman in his arms, clinging to him like a lifeline.

But their backup plan didn't involve following this track — the only way in or out of El Lobo's compound by ground — for long. There was too much likelihood of their meeting opposition or of El Lobo's men setting up an ambush.

"Coming up on the break point," Diaz yelled over the engine noise, "hold on tight."

Jack braced his legs and tightened his arms around Ari, lifting her slightly off the jeep's floor. She'd be much more cushioned by his body than the hard metal when Diaz slammed the jeep into a hard right turn, rocketing off the track and through the jungle a short way before the undergrowth just became too thick and they could go no further.

"What's happening?" Ari asked as the jeep's engine died and they were suddenly surrounded by a thick, near-palpable silence, the jungle wildlife stunned into momentary quiet by the shocking noise of their arrival.

"We have to leave the vehicle," Jack told her, as the other three leaped out of the jeep. "We can't stay on the road. Too high a risk of ambush." He helped her stand up, hopped down out of the jeep and reached up to lift her down, frowning as he took in the impractical dress she was wearing. "Hunter," he turned his head.

"Yes, sir?"

"I need your change of clothes. You're closest to Miss Monterro's size."

Hunter started digging in his pack, and a few seconds later handed over a rolled pair of jungle camouflage pants, a pair of socks and a shirt.

“Turn your backs,” Jack ordered, and all four men immediately did so, raising their guns to their shoulders and peering out into the jungle, as though to repel attack.

Touched, Ariana nevertheless wasted no time stripping off the hated dress and yanking on the pants and shirt, ignoring the pain in her wrists in favor of speed. She might not be a soldier, but it was still obvious that they needed to move as fast as possible if they were to evade El Lobo and his men.

Jack was quite correct that Hunter was closest to her size, but since the soldier was still a lot broader and a good four inches taller than she, the clothes were huge on her. She did her best, rolling up the pants legs and the shirt sleeves, putting her shoes back on.

“I need a belt,” she said. There was no way the pants were going to stay up, otherwise.

Jack pulled his knife again, turned around and picked up the discarded dress. "We'll make some use of this."

Seeing him cut it to pieces was quite viscerally satisfying, Ariana discovered. She accepted the length of fabric he handed her, threaded it through her belt loops and tied a knot at the front. She probably looked utterly ridiculous, she was well aware, but she was a lot better equipped for a trek through the jungle now than she had been five minutes earlier. Especially when Jack handed her a spare pair of NVGs and helped adjust them to fit her head.

"Have you used these before?" he asked quietly.

"No." The world looked weird, green and bright, but she could see a whole lot better now. The NVGs were heavy, though; she hadn't expected that. They were nothing compared to the weight she knew the men would be carrying, however, so she held her head up and didn't complain.

"Where are we going?" she asked. "Actually, just as much to the point, where are we? Is this even Guàlize?"

Jack smiled; she could see more of the shape of his face now. "Yes, we're still in Guàlize; about thirty miles north-east of Tiaxana."

"Oh."

That actually wasn't so good. Tiaxana was one of the cities in Guàlize where the government held least sway, and thirty miles north-east of Tiaxana put them dangerously close to the Venezuelan border. Ariana went through the geography in her head, made a face. They couldn't risk a border crossing. This was a very unsafe, lawless area on both sides of the border, despite strenuous government efforts from both countries.

"You do have a plan, though?"

"Of course. We're splitting up to confuse anyone tracking us. All four of us have different secondary extraction points; we pre-arranged them with our commanding officer back in the States if we failed in the primary escape plan with the helicopter. He will pass those co-ordinates on to your father to arrange for our extraction when the time comes."

"To avoid a possible leak of the information and El Lobo's men being there ahead of you," Ariana realized.

"Correct. And to avoid possible compromise if any of us get captured, none of us know the others' planned destinations." Turning to the other three Rangers, he said quietly, "Good luck."

"You too, sir," three nods answered him before they were gone, melting quickly into the darkness.

"Thank you!" Ariana called after them, realizing she'd never even known their names, apart from Hunter. He was the one who turned to give her a swift salute before vanishing after the others.

"So," she looked back at Jack, "I guess I'm with you."

"You are. We need to get away from the vehicle, but we'll stop soon and I'll take a look at your wrists."

“I am a doctor, you know,” she said, suddenly feeling a bit peeved with him.

“Yes, and I’m assuming you’re the one who bandaged your arm, since it’s not pulled tight enough. Doctor or not, bandaging your own wrists is impossible to do correctly by yourself.” A massive hand curled gently around her elbow, and she found herself walking, eased swiftly away from the jeep.

Jack had put his left hand on Ariana, using his right to wield the machete he’d drawn from his pack, cutting only where he had to in order to minimize signs of their passage. After a couple of minutes she pulled away from him slightly, determined not to be a burden and slow them down any more than she inevitably would.

“It’ll be easier if I follow you.”

She was right, but Jack really didn’t like having her out of his sight, even if she would be right behind him. “Stay close,” he said after a brief hesitation. “Within arm’s reach. Any problem, yell out at once.”

Ariana nodded acknowledgment and was careful to stay close, trying to put her feet where Jack placed his. The night-vision goggles messed with her depth perception, she quickly found; she had to concentrate on where exactly she was putting her feet. The strain began to tell and before long she could feel a headache beginning behind her eyes. She had no intention of complaining, though, just plodded doggedly along behind Jack. It wasn't until a whippy branch snapped back and caught her sore left wrist that she made a sound of protest.

"Are you okay?" Jack turned at once, in time to catch her nursing her arm.

"Fine," she said, but it came out much closer to a sob than she would have liked, and he didn't miss the distress in her tone.

"Time for a break, anyway."

"I can keep going..."

"Ari, it's time to take a break. I'm your chief protection officer right now. I'm sure Elliot taught you about this."

Never, ever argue with your chief protection officer, Elliot had drilled into her. *It's not only your life on the line if you do.*

"Okay," she acquiesced quietly.

Jack nodded, turned to look for a good spot. He didn't exactly have many options at the moment, but at least they were on reasonably dry ground, under thick cover. A few moments with the machete and he had a bed of thin springy branches laid down. "Here, sit here."

Ariana sank down gratefully, pulling her knees up and resting her chin on them. Jack crouched down beside her, shrugging his pack off.

"Water with electrolytes," he said succinctly, holding a canteen to her lips. "Drink it all. How long since you ate or drank something?"

"I had a bottle of water and some quesadillas shortly before you arrived," she assured him. "I'm good."

"Drink all of this anyway, and here's a protein bar. You'll need your strength." He pressed the wrapped bar into her hands.

"How far do we have to go?" she asked, carefully unwrapping the bar and taking a bite as he began digging around in his pack.

"About six miles."

She made a face, knowing what he knew; that six miles in the jungle on foot would take many long, difficult hours to traverse. He was quite right, that she'd need her energy. Taking a bite of the protein bar, she chewed on it slowly, sipping on the electrolyte-laced water.

Jack found the medical kit and settled to sit beside Ariana, opening the kit across his lap and removing a bandage. Stripping off his gloves, he requested "Give me your left hand, please?"

She obeyed, swallowing the bite of protein bar and saying "I was trying to stab El Lobo. He hit me on the wrist with his gun; I think I might have a fracture. It's a very localized, but stabbing pain."

Jack cursed under his breath, probing with gentle fingers. She hissed as he found the spot.

"I need to feel it properly," he said apologetically.

"I know. Go ahead." She gritted her teeth.

"No actual break and no lump on the bone," he told her, a few agonizing seconds later. "If there's a fracture, it's hairline; you'll need an X-Ray to diagnose."

"Got a machine in that giant pack of yours?"

That made him chuckle. "I'm afraid not. Best we can do is immobilize."

"Except that I may need to use it, so no, thank you. Just wrap it tightly."

He hesitated. "I don't have any painkillers except for morphine..."

"Definitely not. Just wrap it, Jack."

She was going to be in pain, and there was absolutely nothing he could do about it. Gritting his teeth with frustration, Jack set to wrapping her wrist firmly, working from her hand right up to her elbow and then back down again. Ari watched in silence, chewing on her protein bar, so he had to assume that he was doing the job to her satisfaction.

"The other wrist?" he asked once he'd finished.

"That's bruised, maybe a slight sprain. He twisted my arm up behind my back to force me to stand still for the photo to be taken."

A hot spike of rage in Jack's gut made his lips curl up in a snarl. He forced himself to keep his voice steady as he moved around to Ariana's other side and took her right hand in his to begin unwrapping the bandage.

"Any pain in your elbow or shoulder?"

"No. He didn't wrench it up too high, it was just a crusher grip on my wrist. I — I could feel the bones grating together." Ariana found herself suddenly shaking. "He was so strong. I couldn't get away." Her voice trembled.

There was no way Jack could let that pass without comforting her. Carefully placing her hand down on her lap so as not to jar it, he put his arm around her, pulling her gently against him, pressing her face into the warm curve of his neck.

"You're safe now, Ari, I promise. Nobody's gonna hurt you, and if I ever lay eyes on that bastard I'm gonna kill him."

He sounded both deadly serious and fiercely protective. Shivering, Ariana allowed herself the luxury of being held in the comforting embrace for a minute or two before reluctantly pulling back.

“Finish bandaging it, please, Jack,” she held her arm up to him again. “We need to move.”

She was being brave as hell; his heart swelled once again with love for her.

“I’m gonna get you out of this,” he told her, his voice calm and evenly reassuring as he began to wrap her wrist tightly. “I’m gonna get you safely back to your father. No matter what.”

Walking through the jungle at night was exhausting and very frightening, even wearing the night-vision goggles. Before long Ariana had a pounding headache and was aching in every limb, not just her injured arms, but she stuck doggedly to Jack’s heels, determined not to be a hindrance.

Unfortunately, the shoes she was wearing, while they'd been better than the ghastly stilettos The Black Wolf wanted her to wear, weren't really suited for a jungle trek, unlike Jack's heavy combat boots. Even trying to walk in his footsteps eventually did her no good, as she finally caught her toe under a thick jungle vine and tripped, crashing headlong to the ground with a pained scream as she instinctively threw her arms out to break her fall.

"Ari!" Jack was at her side in an instant, lifting her back to her feet. "Easy. Easy. Did you hurt your arms?"

There was a constant, throbbing ache up both arms and her head was pounding with pain. She was working so hard on choking back the sobs that she couldn't get a word out.

"All right. Time to rest." She'd reached her limits, Jack recognized, and he silently cursed the fierce independence that had kept her from telling him he was pushing her too hard. They were in a bad spot right now, though, thick mud underfoot as they made their way through a swampy, shallow valley between low hills. "Can you stand for just a moment?"

She did, leaning against him while he picked up the machete he'd dropped and sheathed it. "I'm going to carry you. We won't be going too far, hopefully, but I may have to ask you to stand again a time or two."

Barely holding herself together, Ari nodded. "Can I take the goggles off, please?" she managed to ask weakly. "They're heavy…"

"I have them." Carefully removing them, again cussing himself out for not remembering how hard NVGs could be when someone wasn't used to them, Jack tucked them away in his pack. "Dawn's not too far away, anyway," he said reassuringly, picking Ari up in his arms. "I'll find us a good spot and we'll hole up and rest for a few hours before we have to move out again."

All she could do was remain as still as possible to try and make it easy for him, stand up a couple of times when he had to clear a bigger space for them to move through. The throbbing agony in her arms meant she couldn't even hold onto him to [illegible]n. Jack didn't seem to have any issue with [illegible]gh, holding her firmly and forging [illegible]nward.

At last he said; "This will have to do. It's dry, at least."

Ari was so tired she just leaned against a tree and watched as he again cut branches, weaving them swiftly into a thin mat. It took her a few moments to realize that she could see him, a thin gray light beginning to filter through the trees heralding the dawn and illuminating his powerful figure as he worked.

"It's daylight," she said numbly.

He pulled off his NVGs, looked up. "Soon. It's all right. We can get a few hours rest before we move on."

Watching him move around, efficiently binding together three saplings and laying foliage over the angled trunks to make a shelter, time seemed to fall away for Ariana. She'd never seen him like this, had only ever seen him in field uniform the one time, when he'd rescued her from the kidnappers who had killed her mother. Always after that he was wearing dress uniform or a suit and tie, and while those had suited him very well with his height and breadth of shoulder, he looked utterly in his element right now, face streaked with camouflage makeup, building a shelter in the jungle for her to rest.

She wasn't going to be comfortable, was all Jack could think. She looked exhausted, bruised... almost any position would be painful for her to lie in except flat on her back, and he couldn't see that working out, in the small space he'd managed to build. Looking around, his eyes fell on his pack. He could settle her against that, for a while.

"Here," he held out his hand to her, and she came to him slowly, walking with exaggerated care, as though she was afraid she might fall at any step. Carefully, he lowered her to sit against the pack. "Don't fall asleep just yet. You need to eat, first."

She sighed, but nodded, and he reached for the ration packs he'd set aside. "It's not going to taste real good. I can't risk a fire to warm it."

"Don't care."

Her eyelids were drooping, so he moved quickly, ripping open the MRE. "Get this down and there's a small piece of chocolate for afterward," he bribed, placing the squeeze pack into her hands and indicating she should suck from the plastic spout.

Ariana smiled wearily. "You know I'd kill for chocolate," she tasted the MRE, made a face.

"I remember," Jack said quietly.

Tawny-brown eyes lifted to his.

"Eat," he turned away finally, unable to meet her gaze, and reached for his own ration pack.

She obeyed, her tired mind unable to comprehend why he would remember so much about her. They'd spent a week together six years ago, a week where she'd clung to him in terror, just a scared young girl imprinting on the man who'd carried her out of a terrible situation. Yes, they'd spent one heavenly night in each other's arms, but after that he'd left, and she hadn't seen him since.

"Here," Jack said quietly, and she looked up to realize that she'd managed to finish the

MRE, and he was holding two small, wrapped squares of chocolate out to her.

He's given me his own piece, she thought vaguely, but hell, it was chocolate, and she was most definitely not too proud to take it.

"Thank you," she mumbled, reaching to take them, but her arms hurt like hell and she couldn't make her fingers work to open the wrapping. Jack took them back from her wordlessly, unwrapped the first and held it to her lips.

That was a mistake, he recognized instantly, I should have put it back in her hand... huge eyes looked up at him, her soft lips brushed his fingertips as she took the treat, and Jack was suddenly ragingly, achingly hard for her despite his own weary body.

Taking a deep breath, he unwrapped the second piece of chocolate and again held it to her lips, knowing very well he was playing with fire, but unable to stop himself.

She whispered his name this time just before she took the chocolate from his fingers, and his free hand lifted to touch her tangled hair gently. Ariana leaned into the touch, her eyes closing, long sooty lashes sweeping down to lie on her dirty cheeks. Even with dirt and some of his greasy camouflage facepaint smeared across her face from where she'd pressed it against his neck earlier, Jack still thought she was the most beautiful woman he'd ever laid eyes on.

"We have to rest," he said at last, his voice husky as he broke the electric silence between them.

Ariana nodded, but she couldn't even manage to open her eyes. Jack was still petting her hair gently and it felt so good, she felt so safe this close to him. She heard him sigh, and then he moved around her, laying his rifle and machete close by where he could reach them, sitting down close beside her before strong arms wrapped around her and lifted her into his lap.

"Lean on me," Jack said gruffly. "The pack's too hard, and lumpy."

Jack himself was hard with muscle and wearing bulky body armor which hardly made the softest of beds, but he was blissfully warm, the heat of his body against her back soothing as his arms folded gently around her. He lifted her sore wrists and placed them carefully across her body before he put his large, warm hands over her own.

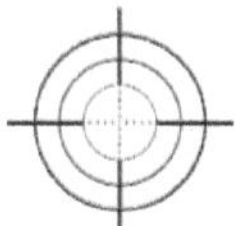

Her head fell sideways against his chest almost instantly, her whole body going limp as her consciousness slipped away. Jack, though, sat staring into the slowly brightening jungle, about as far from sleep as it was possible to get.

Nothing's changed. Six years, and nothing's changed.

One look at Ariana and he'd been lost. At nineteen she'd been a girl still, fresh and lovely as she budded into womanhood. At twenty-five she was a woman in the full bloom of her beauty, stunning enough to turn any man's head, but it had never been just her beauty that attracted Jack. Her courage, her determination and inner strength had been there even as she tried to hold herself together through the tragedy of her mother's murder, but today he'd seen just how indomitable she really was. Jack had known soldiers who couldn't have handled the trek Ariana had made tonight, not injured and in inappropriate shoes and ill-fitting clothes.

He'd half-thought Ariana might not even remember him, but her shocked gasp of his name had put paid to that idea. The way she'd snuggled trustingly against him in the jeep, had leaned into his touch just now, made it impossible for him to just walk away this time.

If, that is, he could get her back to Guàlize City alive.

Chapter Nineteen

Ariana blinked awake to Jack's low voice calling her name. Her eyelids felt crusty with sleep; it was a huge effort to peel them apart. Slowly, the jungle around her came into focus, and at the same time the pain in her arms returned with a vengeance.

"Oh, God, it wasn't just the mother of all terrible dreams," she croaked. Something brushed the side of her brow lightly — had Jack just dropped a kiss there?

"I'm sorry," he said quietly. "I wish I could tell you that it was."

"You being here is about the one bright spot in it," she said honestly, all her filters gone with exhaustion and pain. Jack stiffened a little, then sighed.

"I'm here, Ari. I'll always be here if you need me." Carefully he shifted, lifting her off his lap. "I'm gonna risk a small fire, make a hot drink."

She lay limply back against his pack, watching as he efficiently made a small pit lined with stones before building a tiny fire of dry sticks and lighting it with a fire starter from his belt pack.

"The coffee's terrible," Jack said, obviously aware of her watching him, "but the caffeine kicks like a mule."

"Sounds good," Ariana said honestly. She had no plans to complain about how awful she felt; she suspected he knew anyway.

"I've only got one cup..."

"I really could not care less. Gimme." The coffee even smelled bad, and Jack was right, it tasted terrible. She made a face as she sipped. "Could you not even buy reasonable instant coffee?"

"It actually is reasonable instant coffee. It's the purifiers I had to chuck in the water that make it taste so bad." Jack busied himself preparing food while she drank. “At least we can have hot food now.”

“Aren’t you worried about the smoke being spotted?” Ari looked up, to where the thin smoke from the fire trickled up towards the tree canopy high above them.

“Not really, no. It’s a hot day, the jungle will give off a lot of vapor. We’d be in much more danger of being spotted at night.”

She nodded in understanding, accepting the pouch of food he gave her. “And this is...?”

“Honestly, don’t worry about the flavor. They all taste bad, but they’re slightly better warm than cold.” Jack flashed her an unexpectedly broad smile, white teeth flashing in his filthy face. “I’ve got more chocolate for afterwards,” he waved the small packages in her direction.

“Bribery will get you everywhere, when you’re using chocolate as an incentive,” Ariana had to laugh at his gleeful grin. “Ugh, even convincing me to eat this,” she almost choked on the first mouthful. “Oh my God. Was I just too exhausted to notice how horrible this was last night?”

“Probably.” Jack’s grin was wry. “It was cold then, too.”

“That would be worse, yeah.” She made herself swallow it all, though, washing it down with sips of the bitter coffee, and nearly snatched Jack’s fingers off grabbing for the chocolate when he offered it. He laughed quietly at her eagerness as he kicked dirt over the fire and gathered up the packaging from their food, stowing it carefully in his pack.

“I’m just gonna get some more water. There’s a little watercourse we crossed about a hundred yards that way.” He pointed. “Stay here?”

“Of course.” She was hardly fool enough to go wandering off into the jungle by herself. Though, as he disappeared from sight, she did stand up and move behind a tree to relieve herself.

When Jack returned, he found Ariana sitting on his pack, combing her tangled hair out with her fingers, picking out little bits of leaf debris and twigs with a rueful expression on her face as she slowly worked through the mass. When she saw him, she asked;

“I don’t suppose you’ve got anything I could tie my hair back with? I think I yanked a few handfuls out catching it on tree branches last night.”

“Sure,” he dug in a side pocket of his pack, pulled out some paracord and cut a length off for her with his knife.

“Thanks!” She tugged her hair over her shoulder and gathered it in a bundle, wincing as her sore wrists protested the action. Gritting her teeth to ignore the pain, she braided her hair quickly before tying the scrap of cord around the end and knotting it.

Jack’s fingers touched her cheek lightly and she looked up at him curiously. “What is it?”

“The bit here, where he cut it,” he lightly flicked shorter strands hanging over her ear. “It doesn’t go in the braid.”

There was something murderous buried in his expression that made her say “It’s only hair, Jack. It’ll grow back.”

“I’m still gonna hunt him down and kill him for laying a fuckin’ finger on you.” His voice was quite calm and steady, his expression unchanging. The words, a simple statement of fact. “But first, let’s get outta here. Your father’s waiting.”

“Okay.” Getting to her feet, suppressing the groan that threatened to escape as her aching muscles protested, Ariana smiled bravely at Jack. “So where are we headed?”

“The lake. Lake Maracaibo,” when she frowned at him in puzzlement. “We’re not far from the southern tip. We’ll stay on the right side of the border, but there are regular coast guard patrols. Even if we miss our scheduled pickup, we’ll be fine.”

She wished she could share his confidence, but as he shouldered his pack and set off through the jungle again, Ariana squared her shoulders and followed in his large footsteps. Jack would get her out of this, she had to believe that. One way or another.

They were fording another shallow watercourse — the ground was getting lower and boggier as they approached the lake, making the going even more difficult — when Jack looked up sharply.

"What is it?" Ariana asked, then heard the noise herself. "Is that..."

"A helicopter. Come here." He pulled her close to the trunk of a large tree. "Crouch down, hug your knees. Curl up small." He demonstrated, close by, and she nodded and obeyed.

"Why?" she asked as the sound of the rotor blades grew louder; closer.

"If they have infra-red — and there's not much point in trying to search for us in the jungle unless they do — then the operator will be trained to pick out human shapes. Crouched down like this, we don't look human, more like wild pigs."

She nodded in understanding. "If they're using infra-red to look for us, that means El Lobo has the local police in his pocket."

Jack flicked her a cynical look before going back to peering up through the trees. "Did you really expect that he wouldn't?"

“I hoped,” she said, a little sadly.

“You father and his friend the President have done so much, Ariana,” Jack said gently, seeing her downcast expression. “But it can’t be done all at once. They’ve only been trying to clean up for a decade or so; before that they were fighting the system from the bottom up, it was too hard. Ten years isn’t nearly long enough to root out every corrupt bureaucrat — and even decent ones will still co-operate if his loved ones are threatened.”

“That’s true,” she admitted.

The sound of the rotor blades had passed over, though Jack could still hear them in the distance. He was pretty sure the hunters were searching in a grid pattern, which meant at any time he and Ariana could cross over into the next square in their search grid.

“Come on. We need to move. During the hot day, it’s much harder to distinguish details,” he explained as he and Ariana made their painstaking way onward through the thick jungle undergrowth. “At night, a human shape is a lot more distinct, easy to pick out even if we do hunker down when we hear them coming."

"So we need to reach the lake before nightfall?" Ariana asked.

"Our pickup is due about an hour before sunset, local time. They'll make another pass by about three hours later. After that we're on our own."

That was a very scary thought, even though she had full confidence in Jack; the thought of having to try and hail a patrol boat with no idea if the men aboard would be loyal to the government or bought by El Lobo's dirty money. Ariana swallowed and nodded.

"How far do we still have to go?"

"A little bit more than two miles."

She winced. Two miles of swampy, boggy jungle might as well be twenty on flat, open ground. It was going to be a long, hard day, and she already ached in every muscle. "Then I guess we'd better get moving," she said bravely.

"Good girl," Jack said, and there was no condescension in his expression as he glanced back at her, only admiration for her courage. Ariana gave him a determined nod.

They heard the helicopter coming close again a little more than an hour later; this time Jack told Ari to hunker down where she was while he moved a little ways off, so they didn't always appear to be in really close proximity.

It was a lot more frightening, crouching down alone in the jungle, listening to the rotors getting closer and closer until the tree canopy above her shook with the down wash from the blades. Ari tucked her head between her knees and tried to breathe steadily.

"It's fine. They're going to go away," she told herself. She could feel her heart beginning to hammer in her chest again. No. No panic attacks now.

"Phalanges. Metatarsals. Cuneiform bone, navicular bone, cuboid bone, talus, calcareous, fibula, tibia..." the familiar names steadied her, calmed her. "Patella, femur..."

"Ari," a gentle hand touched her back. "Ari, it's safe. They're gone."

Jack's heart broke for Ariana as she lifted her head slowly. He'd heard her murmuring to herself, but couldn't hear what she was saying until he crouched right down beside her. The steady litany was clearly a coping method she used to stave off a panic attack; the measured cadence of her voice told him she was succeeding, but they didn't have time for her to complete her little ritual.

"Are they gone?" she asked, looking up at him, where he knelt in the dirt at her side.

"Yes. But we have to move. They're intensifying the search. We have to get to the lake quickly, so that I can scout and make sure our extraction point isn't compromised even before our pickup arrives."

"Okay." Straightening up, taking a deep breath, she followed him into the jungle again. After a few minutes, though, he heard her soft voice, turned to see if she was speaking to him.

Ariana froze in the middle of saying metacarpals. “Sorry. I’m just…”

“It’s alright,” Jack said. “I thought you were speaking to me. Carry on.”

He knew what she was doing, obviously. “I started doing it while studying pre-med,” she rushed out as they started moving again. “After — not long after the last time I saw you. I used to get panic attacks, regularly. I saw a psychologist; he seemed to want me to pray, but I couldn’t; not after Mama. I spent too much time praying while we were hostages, and God did not answer me.”

Jack winced, though he said nothing. Ariana wanted to tell him, and so he listened as she carried on.

“So I started using the bones of the human body as a concentration mantra. I had to learn them anyway for exams; nobody thought anything of it that I used to walk around muttering them under my breath. After a while, the panic attacks went away.”

“They never really go away,” Jack said shortly. “You just learn to cope.”

"You?" Ariana sounded astonished.

"Yeah," he glanced back at her, saw her looking at him with interest. He reached up to finger the thin white scar that curved from his lower lip, down through his two days' growth of beard, onto his neck. "I never told you how I got this, did I?"

She shook her head, intrigued.

"Roadside bomb, in Afghanistan. The vehicle I was in overturned. The Colonel, Captain Cullane as he was then, he was in the transport behind, with Elliot. They both left their vehicle to come and pull us out. Risked their lives, because everyone knew the roadside bombs were traps. There were always snipers there ready to pick off anyone who moved."

"Oh, no," shocked, she put a hand to her mouth. "They were shooting at you?"

"Yep. I was barely conscious, bleeding out, and I was the only one left alive in my vehicle anyway. Elliot and Captain Cullane pulled me out and carried me to their transport. A sniper got a shot in on the captain as they were loading me in. Bullet went clean through his leg. Elliot took the wheel and drove us the hell out of Dodge." Jack smiled a little, as he remembered waking up in the field hospital to find Elliot sitting with his feet up on the end of Jack's bed, reading a book.

"I'm gonna miss him so much," Ariana said quietly.

"Me too," Jack replied, closing his eyes in brief, remembered pain.

"Is Mara all right?"

"No."

"Of course she's not, what a stupid goddamn question," Ariana berated herself. "How will I ever be able to face her?"

"None of this was your fault, Ari." Scrambling over a massive tangle of tree roots, Jack turned to help her over them, grasping onto her elbow rather than taking her by the hand, ever considerate of her sore wrists. "The Black Wolf paid for Elliot's murder, plain and simple, bought his death with cold hard cash. You can't blame yourself for that."

"Paid for because he was guarding me!"

"And if he hadn't been doing that, Ell might not have survived this long. The officer who took over his company was killed by a suicide bomber in Afghanistan two years ago." Jack shrugged.

"That's..." Ariana couldn't comprehend living that way. "Why? Why would you do it? You had the chance to get out six years ago, I know you did, you and Elliot could both have quit..."

"My father was a Ranger," Jack told her. "Noncom — a sergeant. Following in his footsteps was the only thing I ever wanted to do as a kid, but he wouldn't let me enlist at eighteen, made me get my ass through college first."

She'd always known he had to have a college education, that he wouldn't be an officer otherwise, but it had never occurred to her to ask what he'd studied. She did so now, curiously.

"I majored in criminology, actually," Jack replied with a quiet chuckle. "Thought that if the Rangers didn't want me, I might try for the military police."

Ariana smiled at that. "You'd be an excellent policeman, military or otherwise. Criminals would be far too afraid of you to misbehave," she joked.

"If only!"

The sound of the helicopter returning again made Jack swear and push Ari down beneath a big tree. He didn't have time to move away, so crouched right up against her, crowding her into the tree trunk, trying to make them just one large indeterminate warm mass.

Ari found herself breathing fast as Jack pressed against her, putting a long arm around her and tucking her head in under his chin. He was warm, sweating; probably less than her, actually, which was surprising considering he was the one lugging an enormous pack around, but he didn't smell bad. Quite the opposite. He smelled of jungle and an animal musk that sent her head spinning, made her remember the heated night six years ago when he'd taken her virginity and ruined her for any other man all at the same time.

"Jack," she whispered as the rotor blades faded into the distance.

He felt her lips move against his neck, told himself very sternly that this was absolutely not the time to look down at her. But his strength of will always failed him whenever Ariana was near, he'd known that for years. So he looked down at her dirty, tired face gazing up at him, and once again lost himself in her eyes.

"Ari," Jack said huskily, and it was such a short, short distance for their lips to come together. His arm was already around her; he tightened it to pull her closer, shifting to kneel beside her. Ariana's own arms slid up around his neck as she kissed him back, all the stresses of the last few days melting away until they both forgot where they were, forgot their tired, aching bodies and the very real danger they were still in.

It wasn't until Ariana's sore wrists protested her clutching tightly at Jack, her hands clenching in his shirt collar making pain shoot up her arms, that she winced and pulled back. Both of Jack's arms were wrapped firmly around her by now, holding her close, and as she pulled her head back she saw that his eyes were closed, the expression on his face one of pure need.

Slowly, Jack opened his eyes, half-afraid of what he would see when he looked at Ariana. She was studying him silently, her expression unreadable.

"I'm sor-" he started to say, but her finger touched lightly to his lips, cutting him off.

"Don't you dare apologize. We'll discuss this after we're out of this goddamn jungle. Now come on. The light's changing; sunset can't be far off."

Chastened that Ariana had to recall him to his duty, Jack got to his feet, helped her up with a strong hand under her elbow. "You're right." He checked his GPS watch, pulled out his map and traced the co-ordinates on it. "Can't be far now."

"Let's hope not," Ari agreed wearily, trudging on after him. The ground had been horrendously marshy for the last two hours; her shoes and clothes were completely soaked through and covered with mud. The only good thing was that she didn't think the water was deep enough for caimans, the local crocodile species. Not yet, anyway.

"This way," Jack made a turn to angle a little further to the east. "Ground should be a bit dryer up here and we'll come out on a bit of a beach. Not too far now, Ari. Come on. You can do it," he exhorted her, seeing her struggling to pull her foot out of a muddy patch.

"Oh, shit!" Her foot came free with a thick sucking sound, but the shoe didn't. Ariana almost fell, completely off-balance; Jack just got to her in time, catching her and lifting her up.

"I'll get your shoe. Sit there," he plonked her rather unceremoniously on a large fallen tree trunk, not that Ari intended to protest. She watched as he went back to the spot where she'd tripped before rolling up his sleeves and plunging both hands into the mud.

Five minutes later, she said "Jack, we're wasting time. Jack!"

He swore long and loud, standing up with the black mud dripping from his fingers. “You need your shoe, Ari!”

“We need to get to the beach more. It can’t be far, Jack, come on. I can do it.” She stood up.

“Ari, your feet…”

“Are trashed, anyway.” She gave him a small smile. It had taken everything she had to keep from limping throughout the day, when blisters the size of pennies had started springing up on her heels and toes. She didn’t even want to think about the mess she’d find when she finally peeled off her soaked, muddy socks. “We gotta go, Jack.”

He swore again before wiping the worst of the muck off his hands onto his pants legs, unsheathing his machete and striding forward, a murderous expression on his face. Ari couldn’t help a small smile as he took out his anger and frustration on some hapless jungle vines, hacking and slashing them out of the way.

“Just be careful where you put your feet,” Jack said gruffly once he’d cleared a path. “Last thing we need is for you to step on a sharp stick or something."

"Or get bitten by a water moccasin," Ariana said helpfully. He cast her a fulminating glare.

"Don't, Ari, this isn't funny!"

"Doctors do have the most inappropriate sense of humor, I've been working on developing mine," she said to his retreating back before sighing and following in his wake.

Chapter Twenty

They'd only progressed a short distance further before Jack gave a shout of triumph. "I see it, there's a break in the trees! It has to be the lake!"

Exhausted, Ari still managed to smile at him when he turned to her, grinning exultantly. "You did it, Jack. You got us here."

"You got here all on your own two feet, don't give me any credit for that. Come on, sweetheart. Not far to go now." She was limping now, her shoeless foot obviously very painful — actually it was more of a hobble. Jack suspected she had hellish blisters, wished he could carry her; but it would be literally impossible, not with the machete to handle to get them through the jungle, and the need to be able to easily get a hand on his gun at all times as they went out into the open.

“Are we at the right co-ordinates?” Ari asked, catching up with him. Jack checked his watch.

“Nearly. Less than a half mile away, but it’s quite a good-sized beach area here, from the map...”

“Not so much,” she warned a little disparagingly. “Maracaibo’s beaches are more on the eastern shore, the Venezuelan side, and up around the mouth of the lake. It’ll be stony here if anything.”

“Still easier going than the jungle, because I can carry you if I don’t have to use the machete.” He slashed away another thick curtain of vines, and now Ari could see the break in the trees too, a very clear break, orange light bright ahead of them.

“That looks suspiciously like sunset. You’d better go on ahead, try and hail the boat in case they leave without us,” she warned.

“Absolutely not.”

Ariana blinked.

"If you think I'm letting you out of my sight for more than five seconds, you've got another think coming," Jack's voice was calm and quite steady. "No, Ari. I told you, the pickup was due an hour before sunset; we probably already missed it. They'll make another pass about two hours after darkness falls. We'll wait."

She sighed wearily, but nodded in agreement, slogging onward.

The sun was right on the horizon when they finally emerged from the edge of the jungle onto, as Ariana had suggested, a rocky shoreline. The stones were smooth, water-polished, some of them thickly coated in a slimy green algae — and the whole place smelled appalling, like rotting vegetation and fish.

"West from here," Jack said, sheathing the machete. "Come here, I'll carry you..."

"No, I'm fine," Ariana insisted. "This is duckweed; it covers large parts of the lake. It's slippery when it's washed up on the shore like this at low tide. If you slip carrying me, we'll both go down."

He couldn't really argue with her; made a face. "All right. But stay close, then I can catch you if you fall."

She had no intention of straying more than a step from his side. At that moment a single step felt like it would be beyond her physical capabilities, but she told herself that she could do it. One foot in front of the other, one step at a time.

Jack's strong hand wrapped around her bicep as she moved forward. "On second thoughts, maybe I'll just hold onto you."

"I'm okay with that," Ariana glanced up at him with a weary smile. The single shoe she was still wearing wouldn't have nearly the grip of his heavy combat boots, and her light weight made it far more likely that she would slip. Especially when she wasn't watching her footing; her feet went out from under her almost instantly and she was only saved from a hard landing on her butt by Jack's firm grip on her arm.

"Whoa, this is even slipperier than I expected!"

"Take it steady. I told you, we've got at least a couple of hours to wait, but let's try and get as close as we can before the light goes completely. This will be even more treacherous going in the dark."

She couldn't argue with that, and though they had to go slowly, picking their footing carefully, it was at least a little faster than moving through the jungle.

"Around here," Jack said finally, and she was very grateful for it because she could barely see the stones under her feet any more. He peered out over the lake, looking for a boat, but could see little except the lights from the Venezuelan city of Ciudad Ojeda, over thirty miles away on the lake's north-eastern shore.

"Do we wait here?" Ariana asked quietly.

"No," Jack decided. "We'll get off the shoreline, for now. Come back about a quarter hour before pickup is due." He led her back towards the edge of the jungle. "I want to take a look at those feet of yours."

Ari winced at the thought, but didn't have much choice, not with his firm grip on her arm. They ended up sitting on a big fallen tree just a few feet back into the concealing jungle, and Jack handed her a protein bar before pulling a penlight from one of his apparently infinite pockets.

“Let’s have a look.”

“Do I have to?” she asked, but sighed and twisted sideways to put one foot into the hand he held out implacably.

Jack was very gentle as he peeled off her sock, but he still heard Ariana’s breath hiss between her teeth and knew what he found wouldn’t be pretty.

“Oh, Ari,” he said softly when he’d finally peeled the material away and shone his penlight on the small, delicately-boned foot beneath.

“It’s not that bad,” she lied stoutly.

“It is that bad, and you’re going to need hospital treatment when we get out of here.” There was little he could do right now other than gently clean the weeping blisters with an alcohol wipe and use another bandage to re-wrap her foot as best he could. He at least had a pair of clean, dry socks in his pack and could get those out for her. "Now the other one."

This foot was the one with the shoe on it; the laces were a knotted lump of dried mud it took Jack a good couple of minutes to pick free.

Ariana clenched her teeth as Jack started to pull the shoe off, fighting to keep down the scream of pain that wanted to emerge. She suspected this shoe had only stayed on because it had been a little tighter than the lost one, and consequently her blisters were actually worse.

Jack hissed with horror once he'd finally removed the sock underneath. "Why didn't you say something earlier, Ari? We could have stopped to treat these..."

"And maybe missed the second pickup? No, thanks," she said firmly. "We wouldn't have traveled any faster."

"But you must have been in so much pain!" He could hardly bear to think of it, Ariana soldiering on through the jungle in absolute agony, not even saying a word. "You're not a soldier, Ari, you shouldn't have to bear this..."

“Shh,” she reached out, gently brushed his stubbled cheek with her fingertips. “It’s all right, Jack. The boat is gonna be here soon and everything will be fine.”

In the dim light reflected by the penlight, she could see indecision on his face. “What is it?” she asked astutely. “What are you thinking?”

“I’ve got two syrettes of morphine...”

“No.” It was a very definite negative. “No, Jack. Not now. Once we’re safe on the boat, I’ll think about it, but not now. I won’t be a burden to you.” The morphine might help with the pain, but it would also leave her unable to think clearly, or help Jack if he needed her.

“You could never be a burden.” His big fingers curled gently around hers and he squeezed lightly. “Never.”

She smiled at him, and they gazed into each other’s eyes in the fading light for a moment before Jack visibly shook himself.

“Last bandage,” he took it out of his first-aid kit. “No more injuries, all right?”

“I’ll try not to,” she promised, watching as he gently cleaned and then wrapped her foot.

"Just hand me the socks. I'm not putting that shoe back on."

"I'll carry you to the boat, when it comes," Jack promised, and she didn't argue the point.

Once Jack had tended her feet as best he could manage and carefully rolled his own spare socks on over the bandages, he handed Ariana his water canteen. "You'd better finish it off."

They'd been drinking throughout the day, Jack regularly refilling the bottle whenever he found reasonably clear water and adding purification tablets. Ariana was used to the slightly chemical taste by now, drank without complaint as Jack picked up the packaging from the bandages and wipes.

"How much longer?" she asked after he sat down beside her on the tree trunk again, clicking the penlight off to save the battery.

"About an hour until we need to move," he checked his watch. "Lean on me, Ari. Get a little rest, if you can. I'll keep watch."

If he'd thought she would turn down the offer, he was very much mistaken. Ariana promptly snuggled close, grabbed his wrist and pulled his arm around her, leaning her head against his broad chest. Startled, Jack stiffened for a moment before chuckling quietly and hugging her closer.

"You're taking me at my word there, huh."

"It's not your gun hand," she pointed out, closing her eyes.

Smiling, Jack leaned down and pressed a light kiss to her brow. "How you've kept your sense of humor throughout this ordeal amazes me, Ari."

"I told you, doctors are known for a weird and morbid sense of humor," she replied without opening her eyes. "I'm just getting into practice."

Silence fell between them, a soft, comfortable kind of quiet, as they listened to the sounds of the jungle all around them. Jack absently slapped at something biting his neck; while he'd regularly plastered both of them with the military-grade bug repellent from his kit, some bugs just didn't seem to darned well care. Ariana didn't stir as he moved, and he thought for a moment that she'd fallen asleep.

Until she asked "Why did you leave, Jack?"

He froze like a deer in the headlights. "You know why," he replied quietly, after a tense, trembling moment in which he felt like the whole world held its breath. "You were my principal — and you were nineteen, and grieving; emotionally compromised, of which I took advantage. If I had stayed, your father would have found out and he'd have fired my ass anyway."

"Maybe," Ariana allowed.

"Definitely. Your father is a very astute man." Which was the understatement of the year, Jack thought wryly. "He'd have been right to fire me, too. I should never have laid a finger on you. It was utterly wrong and the biggest mistake I've ever made."

Ariana went completely stiff against him and he realized in the same instant what he'd said. Mentally kicking himself, he realized that the only choice he had left now was complete and total honesty.

"With that said, I've never been able to get that night out of my mind," he said, his voice low and soft. "Never been able to get you out of my mind, and I knew that would happen, Ari. If I'd stayed, I would have compromised your safety, because I wouldn't have been able to do my job properly. And I wouldn't have been able to live with myself if anything happened to you."

She didn't say anything, still probably seething with rage from his clumsy words, so Jack made himself carry on. "When Mara called and I heard Elliot was probably dead, I couldn't even face the thought that you might be gone too. It was just too much for me to cope with. I had to keep moving, get on a plane and fly down here, but the whole way there was a little voice screaming in the back of my head that I was gonna find my worst nightmare on that mountainside."

Ariana's head shifted; he felt her looking up at him in the darkness. "Of course, you all thought I was dead," she said softly.

"By the time I arrived, your father and the investigators had figured out you and Fuentes were missing, and the investigators found an empty vial of ketamine. It didn't take long for them to come to the correct conclusion. Figuring out where you'd been taken, and by who, was the hard part."

"Tomàs was working for El Lobo. I don't know if he was all along, but he just said it was for the money. He hated me, Jack," Ari shivered, and Jack tightened his arm around her. "He really hated me. And he just didn't seem to give a damn that he'd killed Elliot and Emma and Jonie and Felipe and the pilots. He was a sociopath, I've never met anyone like that, he just didn't care."

Her voice choked up, and Jack realized that she was crying. "Hey now," he said quietly, reaching up his free hand to thumb the tears from her cheek gently. "Don't fall apart on me now, Ari. We're so close to getting out of this."

"I'm so glad you came for me," she sobbed against his shoulder. "I thought you'd come to kill me when you came in with a gun, and then when I realized it was you, there was just this overwhelming sense of relief, I knew you'd save me..."

"I'm not going to let anything happen to you, angel. I promise," Jack vowed, knowing that this time he was in too deep. This time, he wasn't going to be able to just walk away and pretend nothing had ever happened.

Gently he turned Ariana's face up to his and kissed her, long and slow, tasting the salt of her tears on her lips. Her hitching breath steadied as they kissed, small fingers curling in the heavy fabric of his fatigues as she clung to him.

"I love you," Jack whispered finally, resting his forehead against hers. "I loved you six years ago and I've never stopped, Ari."

"Don't you dare leave me this time," she whispered back, and he nodded against her brow.

"I won't."

Ariana was the one who instigated the next kiss, her mouth clinging to his, lips parting to welcome the stroke of his tongue. She startled him by moving, twisting around and swinging her knee over his thighs to sit astride his legs, facing him. He growled low in his chest as she rocked her hips teasingly, pushing her groin against the aching hardness inside his fatigue pants.

“Stop, Ari,” Jack groaned it raggedly at last, pulling his head back. “This isn’t the time or the place.”

“Just you wait until I get you alone with a bed, Jack McAuley, that’s all I have to say,” Ariana replied, making him grin.

“Yes, ma’am. Looking forward to it. I just hope you’ll give me a chance to shower off some of the sweat and stink of the jungle first.”

“I’ll think about it,” she said loftily, making him smile despite his still very real concerns.

His watch beeped suddenly, making them both start, and Jack sighed. “Time to move. Come on.”

Ariana refused to let him carry her, and Jack didn’t press the point. He held her arm in a steadying grasp instead as they put their night-vision goggles back on, picked their way carefully back to the top edge of the stony beach and stood there to wait.

“Is that a boat engine?” Ariana asked after a few minutes.

Jack strained his ears. “I don’t think so. Doesn’t sound right...” the sound was approaching too rapidly, anyway. “Fuck!” Dumping his pack onto the stony beach, he slung his rifle around to his front, quickly checking the magazine. “Ari, it’s a helicopter, run!”

“They might be here for us...”

A cracking sound on the beach stones made her jump.

“They are here for us, they’re shooting at us! Run, Ari!” Jack bellowed. “Get into the trees!”

“What are you going to do?” she grabbed at his sleeve desperately as he took a stride forward.

“I’m gonna try and shoot them down,” he yelled over the terrible noise of machine-gun fire clattering against the stones, coming steadily closer. “Now GO!”

She tried to hang onto him, but he pulled free of her weak grip and sprinted out onto the beach, running at an angle to the incoming fire before dropping to one knee and lifting his rifle, steadying himself.

"Jack!" she screamed helplessly. "NO! JACK!"

Chapter Twenty-One

Bullets clattered ever closer to Ariana, sparking off the stones, and she shook herself out of her temporary paralysis. She wouldn't get far through the trees without Jack, and she didn't want to lose sight of the beach or him, so she started just running along the edge of the jungle as best she could on her sore feet, looking back over her shoulder the whole time. She could see the helicopter now, a white searchlight on its belly brightening the darkness to near-daylight, blinding her so that she had to tear her NVGs off, tracer bullets spitting from the machine-gun poking out through the open side door burning white fiery lines into the night.

She couldn't hear the return rifle fire, could barely make out Jack kneeling on the stones, rifle raised to his shoulder. He had no chance of bringing the chopper down, surely; he was doing this solely as a distraction so that she could get away, hide until the boat came. If the boat came, with the chopper hanging over the beach like that.

Ariana's eyes blurred over with tears again, but she kept stumbling on, fighting to keep going, her breath heaving in her lungs. She couldn't let Jack's sacrifice be in vain; he was offering up his life so that she might escape.

Kneeling on the cold, wet stones, Jack took a deep breath and tried to steady himself, but his fear for Ari rose up in his throat, choking him. If El Lobo got hold of her a second time, there would be no mercy. He would make her suffer for every breath until her last.

Exhaling slowly, Jack squeezed the trigger. The helicopter was turning away from him — they'd lost sight of him when he took off to one side, and frankly they didn't give a damn about him anyway. He was just an inconvenience to be swatted aside so El Lobo could take Ariana back.

Focus. He took another shot. He was hitting the chopper; he could hardly miss at this range, he was a top-grade marksman, but he needed to hit something vital. It wasn't a military chopper so the vulnerable areas wouldn't be armored; if he could just hit an engine or get a clean shot at the pilot he could bring it down, but the damn chopper was turned away from him now. He gritted his teeth before forcing himself to relax his jaw and taking another shot.

"Come on," he said under his breath. "Come on!" He didn't want to switch to full auto, he'd run out of bullets too fast. Another shot.

The helicopter twitched mid-air, and Jack bared his teeth in a fierce grin of triumph. He'd hit the tail rotor. It was still turning but visibly slowing, the craft beginning to auto-rotate. There was a good pilot at the controls; he was going to set it down safely.

Unless, of course, Jack made sure that he didn't.

The machine gun was still spraying fire onto the beach, the shells sparking off stones just feet away, perilously close. Jack sighted in and waited his moment, ignoring the noise, the shards of stone and metal spraying up around him, waiting until the chopper spun back towards him, until he could see the silhouette of the pilot's head as the man fought the failing machine for control.

Breathe in. Breathe out.

Fire.

Ari screamed Jack's name as the chopper seemed to turn back towards him, the machine gun spitting a spiteful rain of deadly metal at him. He couldn't survive that, nobody could survive that!

One moment the helicopter was heading straight for him, the next it was suddenly spinning in mid-air, going up and right over, coming back down in a death spiral towards her. She barely had time to duck and cover her face before it hit the beach nose-first with a terrible, grinding scream of tortured metal on rock, pieces of the rotors shattering off and flying in all directions.

A tremendous BOOM split the night, the shock wave knocking Ari flat on her back. She huddled on the stones, arms wrapped around her head defensively, for what felt like endless minutes as a rain of fiery metal shards fell all around her. Hot tears of loss and terror stung her cheeks, until the sound of someone shouting her name registered and she lifted her head, blinking incredulously.

“Jack?”

“Ari!” he was closer, she could see him running towards her, through still-burning pieces of helicopter wreckage strewn on the beach.

“Jack, I'm here!” somehow she got to her feet, staggered towards him, and a moment later was being caught up in his arms, his face pressed against her throat as he lifted her high in the air.

“Oh God, Ari, you're alive, you're alive...”

"You, too," she choked out, clinging to him, running her hands over his short hair, barely able to believe that he'd somehow survived, had brought the helicopter down, had saved them both.

A movement behind him on the beach made her eyes widen. "Jack!" she screamed, and the note of panic in her voice had him dropping her, grabbing for the pistol holstered on his thigh.

El Lobo Negro had a shattered leg and several broken ribs, but nothing was going to stop him killing the Monterro bitch and the American dog who had stolen her and wrecked his compound. His hand shook as he leveled his gold-plated gun at them. The bitch saw him and screamed; her faithful dog dropped her, whirling, his gun coming up...

Two guns barked at the same moment. Jack heard Ariana scream but he couldn't think of her right now; had to focus on the man with the gun who would kill both of them if he could. He kept pulling the trigger on his pistol until the firing pin clicked on empty and the man lay still.

Only then did Jack spin back around. “Ari?”

She lay, still as death, on the cold wet stones, bright blood blooming on the front of her shirt.

“ARI!” Jack’s terrified roar of rage filled the night.

Chapter Twenty-Two

Ariana woke slowly, blinking tired, heavy eyelids open to see a blessedly familiar face beside her bed.

“Papi?” she whispered.

Raul Monterro dropped the newspaper he was reading and lunged upright, leaning over her even as he punched a call button at the bedside.

“Ariana! You’re awake! Madre de Dios, I thought — I thought we’d lost you!”

She was in a hospital bed, she registered vaguely as a door swung open and a swarm of doctors came rushing in. Her eyes wouldn’t stay open; she fought against the all-consuming lassitude long enough to whisper one important question.

"Where's Jack?"

The grim expression on Raul's face was all the answer she needed. She closed her eyes and let the blackness take her again.

Feverish, confused dreams plagued her; she dreamed that Jack was there, talking to her father, then sitting holding her hand, telling her he was sorry. For what? she wanted to ask him. You saved me.

For leaving you, his ghost told her.

She wept, even in her dreams.

They were giving her morphine, her medically-trained brain assessed the next time she woke. She took her time opening her eyes this time around, lying still and processing the sounds around her first. The beeps of a cardiac monitor were quite expected. Two low voices speaking in the background, not much less so.

“I don’t like morphine,” she said, without opening her eyes. “It makes me see things that aren’t there.”

One of the voices, soft and feminine, came closer. “I understand, Miss Monterro, but it’s also helping you not feel the things that are there. Like the bullet wound that almost killed you.”

“Oh. I was shot?” A number of things suddenly became clearer. Carefully, she opened her eyes, peered up into the smiling face of a female doctor, not too many years older than Ari herself.

“I’m afraid so. I’m sorry, I should have called you Doctor Monterro. I’m Doctor Cardones.”

“I’m a fairly new doctor.” Ari tried to smile. “Can’t exactly treat patients yet.”

“I know, but nevertheless, as one professional to another, I’m going to give it to you straight. You are very, very lucky to be alive. The bullet punctured and collapsed your right lung and transited out through your back.”

Ari's jaw dropped. "How am I alive?" she gaped.

"Fortunately, the boat that was due to pick you up arrived less than a minute after you were shot; they saw the helicopter crash and came straight in. It was a Coast Guard cutter with two fully trained paramedics on board. They kept you going, somehow, until the Army helicopters arrived to evacuate you."

They were too late for Jack, though. Ariana had been trying not to think about him. The tears pricked hard at her eyes, making them feel hot and sore. "Did they get El Lobo Negro?" she asked, trying to distract herself.

"He was already dead when they got there," Dr Cardones assured her. "Captain McAuley," she stumbled over the unfamiliar name, "put thirteen bullets into his head and chest."

Ari couldn't stop the tears, this time. "He saved me," she choked.

"Hush, hush," Dr Cardones reached for the IV tree by the bed, made an adjustment. "You mustn't get distressed, Ariana. Your lung is going to take a while to heal. Just breathe easy."

The blurry blackness swam up on Ariana again. "I really don't like morphine," she slurred out before the blackness overtook her entirely. "I keep seeing Jack."

"What did she say?" Raul asked, coming in just in time to hear the last few mumbled sounds before Ariana slipped back into sleep.

"She doesn't care for the morphine; says it's making her see things that aren't there," Dr Cardones made a note on Ariana's chart. "Regrettably, we don't have a lot of choice at the moment. She has to be kept quiet."

"Was she awake for a little longer this time?" Raul took his customary seat by the bed. "I'm so sorry I missed it."

"I promised you I'd stay with her. You need to eat and sleep just like the rest of us, sir," the doctor reproached him gently. "Ariana was awake for a couple of minutes and seemed quite lucid. I told her what had happened to her and she asked about El Lobo Negro; I told her that Captain McAuley killed him."

"Did she ask for him?" Raul asked.

"No, she became distressed when I mentioned him and began to cry. We can't risk such stress on her lungs, so I had to put her back to sleep."

"All right." Raul reached to take Ariana's hand, stroked her fingers lightly. "Jack will be back soon, baby," he told her softly, wondering if she could maybe hear him in her sleep. "He had a promise to keep."

The folded flag felt heavy as lead in Jack's hands as he knelt to present it to Mara Savige. Elliot Savige hadn't died a Ranger, but that made no difference to his former colleagues. They had turned out in force to give their friend a 'proper send-off' as Lieutenant Hunter called it. Almost every serving member of the Rangers currently in the US filled the cemetery at Arlington to farewell their former brother-in-arms, watching the ceremony somber and silent in their formal uniforms.

“Thank you,” Mara’s face was pale beneath her carefully applied make-up as she looked at Jack, but her eyes were dry. She’d already wept enough tears to fill a river this last week, Jack knew. Selina Cullane sat immediately beside her, a silent symbol of support from the Rangers, just as much as the tightly folded flag Jack, in full formal regalia, had just placed into Mara’s hands. “Thank you for bringing him home, Jack.”

“It was my honor,” he said quietly before standing up, stepping back and offering a formal salute to her. She inclined her head in thanks, clutching the flag closely.

Lt. Colonel Cullane, standing beside his wife, nodded to Jack as he turned to lead the other pall-bearers away.

“Present arms!” Hunter barked, a short distance away, and five current Rangers, including Sergeants Diaz and Mostyn, lifted their rifles to their shoulders to fire the first shot of a three-volley salute.

“It was a good send-off,” Brody Cullane said to Jack as they stood in the officers’ mess later, raising a glass to Elliot's memory. "Ell would have appreciated it."

"He'd have been even more appreciative that we're looking after Mara," Jack said. "Thank you for having Mrs. Cullane stay with her. I know she's needed the support."

"She'll have it for as long as necessary, for life if need be." Brody clapped Jack on the shoulder gently. "So," he said after a moment of silence, "I suppose you're not going to sign those re-up papers I've got sitting on my desk, are you?"

"I'm afraid not, sir."

"Thought so. You've still got six months left."

"Yes, sir."

"I can't just let you go now, you know that."

Jack had known it was coming. He nodded stoically. "I understand, sir."

"However, we've received a request from the Guàlizean government for an experienced officer to assist with training a new counter-terrorism unit they're setting up. They intend to make a push to stamp out the drug cartels once and for all. Quite by coincidence, the skill set they're looking for matches almost perfectly to yours." Brody's tone was dry.

Jack failed to keep the grin off his face. "Is that so, sir? Sounds like an interesting opportunity."

"Quite. I understand Minister for Justice Monterro has personally requested that you review the offer before it's shown to anyone else. The remuneration is quite generous, too."

Bless you, Raul. "Sounds like something I should look into as soon as possible, Colonel."

"We'll be sorry to lose you, Jack," Brody said quietly, removing a sealed envelope from inside his jacket and handing it over. "The Rangers will always be here if you need us, just remember that."

"Thanks, Brody," Jack dropped the formality as he accepted the envelope. Brody nodded with a smile and another clap on the shoulder.

"Best of luck."

He couldn't just hop on a plane back to Guàlize, of course. The wheels of military bureaucracy ground particularly slowly, even with Colonel Cullane doing his best to facilitate the transfer. The Guàlizeans had to set things up on their end, the State Department had to negotiate Jack's status — he ended up with diplomatic immunity, much to his own amusement — a salary commensurate with his new position, and arrange somewhere for him to live. He'd have been quite happy rooming with the embassy guards or staying in a barracks with the men he'd be training, but the diplomats insisted that wouldn't be at all appropriate.

"Whatever," Jack said impatiently to the very efficient lady from the Pentagon who was very patiently explaining to him why he couldn't just head down to Guàlize with nothing but the clothes on his back. "Can you just make it all happen quickly?"

"We're doing everything we can to expedite, Captain," she looked at him over her glasses and handed him yet another form to sign. "I'm sure you have your own affairs to settle here before you leave. A house to sell?"

"I live on-base. Always have." He'd never been one to accumulate belongings, either. Most of his personal possessions had already been packed up and sent on to Guàlize; Raul Monterro was keeping them until Jack arrived. Raul had invited Jack to live at his house, but the State Department had declined on Jack's behalf. He wasn't sure whether to be annoyed about that or not. He wasn't even sure if Ari was going to be there; Raul said that she was still undecided as to whether she would return to the US to take up her residency at Johns Hopkins, or whether she would complete her training in Guàlize.

"Has she asked about me?" Jack asked almost desperately when he spoke to Raul one evening. The other man called most nights to update him on Ari's condition and on how the transfer paperwork was progressing from the Guàlizean end.

"I mentioned your name today and she burst into tears," Raul said. "Doctor Cardones chased me out of the room. Ari's lung is still healing, they don't want her distressed. I think it'll be better if you explain to Ari yourself why you had to go when you get back here."

"It won't be too much longer, I hope."

"That's good. Ariana wants to come home; the doctors are happy to let her go in a few more days as long as she rests quietly at home. I'll have round-the-clock nursing for her, of course..."

"Of course," Jack echoed, knowing how determined Raul was to see Ariana recover as quickly as possible. With the proper medical care, she would recover more quickly at home, it was true. Still, Jack's heart ached that he couldn't be there to take care of her himself. "If talking about me distresses her, don't, Raul. Let her recover in peace. Once I'm there and we can talk, she can decide for herself whether she wants to stay or come back to the US. All I know is that the only thing I can do right now is get myself into a position where we can be together, if Ari so chooses, and this transfer is the only way I can do that."

"I understand," Raul told him, "and you have my full support."

"I don't know exactly when I'll get there, so I suppose you'd better not tell her I'm on my way. If she asks, tell her I'll be there when I can."

"I won't bring the subject up," Raul promised. "Hasta más tarde, Jack. Ven aquí pronto."

"As soon as I can," he agreed before making his own farewells and hanging up.

"I think that's everything, Captain," the administrator said finally, gathering her forms. "Before we let you go, though, there's someone else who wants to speak to you."

He didn't exactly have too many options, so he shrugged and sat back in his chair. The administrator nodded to him as she tucked all the papers into her briefcase and departed; he only had to wait a couple of minutes before the door opened again and a man entered. Dressed in a plain business suit with a nondescript tie, the dark-haired, dark-eyed man looked vaguely familiar. Jack studied him as the other man took a seat.

“I still don’t know your name, but I’m guessing you’re CIA.”

A sardonic grin was his response. “Call me Juan.”

Somehow, he doubted that was the spy’s real name. “I’m surprised to see you back in the US.”

“Well, unfortunately, I had to blow my cover. Minister Monterro and his principal protection agent both saw my face. A spy who’s known by sight to the Minister for Justice is too high a risk, I’m afraid.” Juan shrugged eloquently. “No problem. I can fit in anywhere in South or Central America. Just doing some debriefing here before my next posting.”

“Debriefing, right,” Jack nodded, a sudden suspicion dawning in his mind. “And... recruiting?”

“Well, that’s up to you,” Juan spread his hands. “We know you’re a patriot.”

"And the Guàlizeans are our allies." Jack's tone was cold.

"They are, of course. They still don't tell us everything, and the drug trade has certainly not ended with the death of El Lobo Negro, for which your country thanks you, by the way. Power abhors a vacuum, as the saying goes. An American in charge of training an anti-sicario task force could hear all sorts of useful information."

"And in return?"

Juan's eyebrows rose. "Well, in addition to the princely salary the Guàlizeans have offered you, there would be a stipend, of course…"

"That's not what I'm talking about." Jack shook his head. "I don't want money — as you say, the Guàlizeans are being very generous. What I want is co-operation."

Juan sat back in his chair, an interested expression on his face. "Go on."

"I won't spy for you covertly, either. If I hear any information I think the US could use to fight drug trafficking, I'll share it, but I'll tell Minister Monterro that I'm going to share it. And in return, I want US assistance for anti-drug operations within Guàlize. Not troops or manpower, but intelligence. Satellite images like the ones you gave me, or even better. NSA assistance, real-time, when I ask for it."

"That's an interesting proposition," Juan said slowly, clearly turning it over.

"It costs you nothing, and it benefits everyone," Jack pushed his point.

"I'll have to talk it over with my superiors. It's not something that I can just agree to on my own authority, you understand, especially with other agencies involved. And if you are going to be an overt liaison rather than a covert agent, that means a rethink in your handling."

"Covert really isn't my style."

"We noticed," Juan's tone was very dry. "Considering the mess you made of El Lobo Negro's compound."

Jack's grin was pure pride. "I had help."

"If that's the kind of thing you can do with only three men, I'm really looking forward to see the mayhem you'll wreak on the drug trade." Juan offered his hand to shake. "The very best of luck, Captain McAuley. We won't meet again, but you'll be hearing from my superiors."

"Good luck to you too, Juan, or whatever your real name is," Jack said.

A grin was his only response before Juan departed.

Chapter Twenty-Three

"Hey, m'hija." Ariana looked up to see her father entering her hospital room, a bag tucked under his arm.

"Papi," a smile broke across her face.

"You're awake, and properly this time." He scrutinized the way she was propped up against a mound of pillows, the bed elevated to support her back, before bending to kiss both her cheeks. "And a little color in your cheeks, that gladdens my heart to see it. How are you feeling?"

"Sore," she answered honestly, "but I feel a lot more like myself now I've convinced Doctor Cardones to ease off on the morphine."

"You did?" Raul's brow furrowed.

"Yes. Trust me to know my own limits, Papi. Please." She gave him a wry look. "I am taking painkillers, just not the morphine. I don't like it, I kept seeing things that weren't real." Like Jack, she didn't say, knowing that if she said his name the tears would start again and Doctor Cardones would not take no for an answer.

"All right." Raul sat down in the visitor's chair beside the bed with a sigh, before giving her a smile. "The good doctor says that now you are awake, you need to eat well to regain your strength, and that some treats might not go amiss." With the air of a conjurer performing a stage trick, he produced from the bag he was carrying a large box of Ariana's favorite local Guàlizean chocolates.

Her eyes lit up and she made grabby hands at the box, making Raul chuckle indulgently. He stripped off the cellophane wrapper and handed it over, watching as she made the first selection and popped the sweet treat into her mouth, sighing with pleasure as the chocolate melted on her tongue.

"It is so good to see you smile, m'hija." Leaning forward, he took her hand in his, squeezed it gently, mindful of the bandages covering both her wrists. "I was so afraid I would never see you again."

"Me too, Papi." Right up until the moment she recognized Jack, Ariana had been quite convinced she wouldn't escape alive. She could see the shadows of that same conviction in her father's eyes, pressed back on his hand. "I knew you were doing everything you could to get me back. I believed in you."

Comforted by her little white lie, Raul smiled back at her. "I could not have found you so quickly without Captain McAuley's help; he and his Rangers were very brave..."

"I don't want to talk about it," Ari cut him off.

Concerned at her sudden pallor, the way her lips trembled and her eyes turned shiny with tears, Raul immediately backtracked. "Of course. I'm sorry, m'hija. Let us talk of something else. Must you return to the United States to complete your internship? Without Elliot... well, I am concerned that your safety will be difficult to ensure, there."

Ariana knew what he meant; here in Guàlize it would be far less easy for her father's enemies to target her. Raul planned to run for the Presidency next year, and he deserved to be able to concentrate on his campaign without worrying about her. He deserved her support while he campaigned, too, something that would be impossible if she went back to America.

"We can talk about that, Papi," she said, giving him a small smile as she selected another chocolate from the box. "I must say, the Santa Maria is looking very impressive these days." She gestured around at the well-appointed and equipped hospital room. "Even though this is a VIP suite, Doctor Cardones has been extolling the virtues of the government's new health care programs and what they have done for medical treatments in Guàlize."

"Those reforms were the very devil to get through Congress," Raul shook his head, and just as Ariana had hoped, was diverted into talking about his favorite subject, the political and economic reforms he had dedicated his life to seeing come to pass in the country he loved so dearly. Settling back and savoring her chocolate, she listened to him talk, enjoying just being in his company.

It was about half an hour later when Raul noticed that Ariana's eyes had drifted closed again. Stealthily, he got to his feet, removed the box of chocolates from her lap and slowly reclined the bed again, gently placing her bandaged arms at her sides and tucking the sheet over her.

"Sleep, m'hija," he said softly, bending to kiss her forehead. "Jack will be here soon."

The heat was like a smothering wet blanket slapped straight into his face as Jack stepped off the airplane. He'd taken a commercial flight this time, wearing civilian clothes. He'd even booked his own ticket, although on arrival at the airport in Atlanta he found that someone had obviously pulled strings behind the scenes because his ticket had mysteriously been upgraded to first class.

There was a familiar face waiting for him at the bottom of the rolling stairs. Jack grinned, shouldering the small bag he'd carried on the plane with him.

"Hello again."

"Captain McAuley," Gutierrez gave him a snappy salute. "Good to see you again."

"You too." Jack fell into step beside the Guàlizean agent as they crossed the tarmac. "Where are we headed?"

"Casa Monterro. Miss Ariana is home, as of this morning, and Mr Monterro assumed you would want to see her immediately."

"He's not wrong," Jack agreed as they headed for a black SUV parked beside the terminal. "Uh… do I need to clear Customs?"

Gutierrez gave him a sardonic look. "The official is waiting at the car to stamp your passport. Your luggage will be brought by another of my men who is waiting for it. We're not exactly worried about you smuggling in anything illegal, Captain."

The idea made Jack grin. “You’d better call me Jack,” he offered. “I’m guessing we’ll see a fair bit of each other.”

“Ramón,” Gutierrez said in return as they arrived at the car. There was indeed a Customs official right there, who took Jack’s passport, flicked through to find a blank page, applied a stamp and handed it back with a cheerful;

“Welcome to Guàlize, sir!”

“That’s an efficient way of handling things,” Jack murmured as they climbed into the SUV. “I was fully expecting to go through like any normal passenger and get collected when I came out the other side.”

“You’re not a normal passenger... Jack.”

“Apparently not.” A gate was opened for them to drive out of the airport, the guards manning it waving to Ramón as they passed through.

Ramón didn’t seem inclined to talk, and Jack found himself growing increasingly nervous as they drove through the city. He’d never been the sort to fidget, and military life tended to train one to patience anyway, but knowing that he would see Ariana shortly had him on the edge of his seat, gnawing anxiously on a hangnail.

"Will you sit still?" Ramón barked in annoyance eventually. "You're making me jumpy."

"Sorry," Jack subsided. "I'm just a bit nervous."

"This is the man who jumped out of an airplane in the dead of night to storm a drug lord's compound?" Ramón flicked him an amused look.

"That was different."

"Ah yes, that was combat. This is a matter of the heart."

"Why do I have the terrible feeling you're all watching my every move and just waiting for me to fall flat on my face?" Jack asked dismally.

"Why do I have the terrible feeling you have no idea how to treat a woman? After all, you ran out on Miss Ariana six years ago. I wanted to hunt you down then and kill you, but Mr Monterro said no," Ramón riposted.

Jack froze up completely, his jaw hanging open as he processed the realization that Raul had known for six years that he'd slept with Ariana. Had known, and done nothing. Had allowed him back into the country, had trusted him to lead the search and rescue effort...

"He knew all along how I felt about her."

"A blind man could have seen how you felt about her." Ramón snorted magnificently. " Idiota. The only thing none of us could understand is why you left."

"She was too young," Jack said weakly.

Ramón only rolled his eyes sideways at Jack as they pulled into the driveway and stopped at the gate. Raul's people were a lot more disciplined in their approach to security than the airport guards, Jack noted as the men approached the car cautiously, one of them using a mirror on a long pole to check beneath it for explosives while the other spoke with Ramón. Jack was too busy processing the knowledge Ramón had just so casually imparted, though, to do more than nod distractedly when the two guards wished him welcome before opening the gate and waving them on up the driveway.

"So just remember," Ramón broke the awkward silence as the car drew to a stop, "do not dare to break her heart again."

"I'll try my best," was all Jack could promise. Ramón nodded, clearly satisfied with his promise, and got out of the car.

Jack's heart was pounding as he entered the house, his hands shaking. He couldn't remember when he'd last been this nervous. He dried his sweating palms against his pants legs, straightened the knot of his tie.

"Very handsome," Ramón said sardonically, and Jack scowled at his tone, flipped him the bird.

"Where do I go?"

"I'll take you to Mr Monterro first." Raul gestured Jack to follow him. "He can escort you to Miss Ari... if he wants to."

"You're not helping my nerves," Jack muttered under his breath, but he squared his shoulders and followed Ramón. He'd stared death in the eye plenty of times during his career and never flinched; why he should now be suffering an anxiety attack at the thought of facing Ariana and her father he couldn't fathom.

Raul appeared to share none of Ramón's antipathy, however, rising from his chair with a broad smile as Jack was ushered into his office. "Jack, it is truly good to have you back in Guàlize! I did not dare to hope that we could get you back here so soon!"

"Good to be back," Jack muttered, submitting to the surprisingly enthusiastic hug Raul bestowed on him.

"But what is this? We have talked almost every day and yet now you cannot look me in the eye?" An astute observer, Raul glanced across at Ramón, who pursed his lips and looked out of the window with an innocent whistle. "What has Ramón been saying, eh?"

"Nothing that wasn't true." Jack took a deep breath and looked Raul in the eye. "Six years ago I did something stupid and I didn't stick around to accept responsibility for it."

"Ah," Raul shook his head at Ramón. "Six years ago was a difficult time for all of us, Jack." He gestured Jack to a chair, seated himself.

"You'd just lost your wife, Raul, and Ariana had lost her mother and been through an appallingly traumatic experience; I took advantage!"

"Why do I have the feeling you've been beating yourself up about this for the last six years?" Raul leaned forward, steepled his fingers together in front of him. "Do you know what you did that night, the way I see it?"

Jack blinked. Shook his head slowly.

"You gave her something to think about beside her own grief, and it was precisely what she needed in that moment, comfort that only you could give her. Yes, if you had stayed things might have been different... but I have long since learned to accept that you cannot change the past, only the future." Raul's dark eyes were very intense as he continued "Without your actions, Ariana would have no future."

"That doesn't mean she owes me anything," Jack said quickly.

"Of course not, and Ari would take my head off if I dared to suggest such a nonsensical thing. The debt is mine."

Jack shook his head in denial; Raul wagged a finger at him.

"It is not a debt I can repay. The best I can do is ease your path to happiness with the woman you love; my daughter."

"I do love her," Jack said fervently. "You knew that already, though."

"I did, and I also know how she feels about you."

Jack wanted to ask, but he bit his lip and said nothing. Ariana could tell him herself. Just as he planned to tell her how much he adored her. "May I see her now?" he asked after the silence had dragged into an uncomfortably long minute.

"I'll take you up," Raul said immediately, getting to his feet. "She's waited for you long enough. She cried if anyone so much as mentioned your name, you know."

Jack pressed a hand to his chest as they left the study together, headed up the stairs.

"Please don't. I felt so goddamn guilty leaving, even after the surgeons said she'd pull through okay. But I'd promised Mara I'd take Elliot home."

"You do not have to explain yourself, Jack. Not to me, not to Ariana, not on this matter. Taking Elliot home was of the highest importance. I would have thought much less of you if you had not done so."

"I'm glad you understand, but it still tore my heart out to leave her, especially since I couldn't even say goodbye properly."

They had come to a closed door; Raul stopped and shook his head at Jack. "If you hadn't gone of your own volition, I would have ordered you put on the plane. Tell yourself that if you must, if it will ease your conscience." He stepped back then, a small smile on his lips. "I don't think I need to witness your reunion. I'll leave you to it. Just try not to let her get too agitated. She needs to rest." He left, heading back down the stairs without a backward glance, leaving Jack standing alone outside Ariana's bedroom door trying not to quake in his boots.

He'd run into firefights without hesitation, but turning that door handle was almost beyond him. It took him a good couple of minutes to make his hand close on the smooth metal knob, turn it quietly and open the door.

Jack was already halfway into the room when it occurred to him that he should probably have knocked. Freezing uncertainly, he wondered if he should go back out, but he could see Ari now, lying down apparently asleep, looking like some kind of fairy princess with her silken dark hair spread on the pillow around her, her soft lips parted.

He couldn't take his eyes off her. She'd lost weight, which he supposed was only to be expected. Her cheekbones looked more prominent, her collarbones standing out sharply above the round neck of the vest top she was wearing. Walking quietly closer, he stood gazing down at her, transfixed by the slow rise and fall of her chest, the way her hand lay laxly on the sheet. Slowly, he sank to his knees, placing his hand by hers, not quite touching her, marveling at how delicate her slender golden fingers looked beside his big, rough hand.

He must have made some sound that disturbed her, probably his shoes on the polished wooden floor as he approached the bed, though he'd tried to be quiet. Ariana's eyelashes fluttered slowly before her eyes opened, and she turned her head to look at him.

Jack was utterly unprepared for the broken, agonized look that spread across her face, nor the tears that welled in her big brown eyes.

"No," she said, "not again, please..."

"Ari!" Horrified, he wrapped his fingers around hers.

"You're dead," she almost shouted it. "You're dead, stay out of my dreams!" she tried to pull her hand from his, but he held on tightly.

"What the hell are you talking about?" Jack gaped at her, trying to calm her as she pushed herself to a sitting position. "Ari, I'm fine. You were the one who got shot, not me! Ari! You have to calm down, you'll hurt yourself!" She was struggling against him; afraid for her, he pulled both her wrists into one of his hands, pressed his other one against her shoulder and forcibly pushed her back down onto the bed.

The very real pressure of Jack's strength holding her down snapped Ari out of her panic. She blinked at him, her cries quieting.

"Ari, it's me." He wasn't sure how she'd somehow gotten the impression that he was dead, but the mere thought of how he might feel if the circumstances were reversed had him desperately wanting to comfort her. "It's me, and I'm not dead, I promise you. I never had much more than a few scrapes and scratches. I wasn't with you in the hospital because... well, I had to take Elliott home. I called every day and spoke to your father, I promise. I think I drove him crazy begging him for updates on your condition."

She had finally relaxed, staring up at him wide-eyed, as though she was drinking in the sight of his face. Jack took his weight off his arm, letting go of her wrists with a wince of regret, hoping that he hadn't hurt her too much. She grabbed for his hand, held on tightly.

"Jack." Her voice was so soft he could barely hear it. "Jack, you came back to me..."

"I'm never leaving you again," he promised. "I'm here and I'm staying, for good."

"In Guàlize?" she looked bemused.

"That's right. Your father pulled God only knows how many strings and got me offered a job training paramilitary troops for Guàlize's war on the drug trade. I'm staying, and I'm pretty sure your father hopes that'll be incentive enough for you to decide to stay too, to finish your training here instead of going back to the States."

That made Ariana laugh, tears springing to her eyes again, but this time they were tears of pure joy. "When the two men I love team up to convince me, how could I possibly deny them?"

Jack's rugged face softened. "You love me?"

"Don't you ever doubt it." She put up her hand to stroke his cheek gently. "You're mine now, Jack McAuley. You're on my turf now."

He blinked, laughed. "What will you do, have my passport confiscated if I try to leave?"

“Don’t doubt it.” Ariana’s smile was blindingly happy as Jack gathered her in his arms and pulled her close to claim her lips in a tender kiss.

Chapter Twenty-Four

Ariana had no intention of letting Jack up from the kiss easily, and the way he made a small sound in his throat and gathered her up in his arms, holding her close, told her that he felt just as enthused about their embrace.

A shriek from the doorway made them jump apart, though, Jack whipping around to put himself between Ariana and any potential threat. He didn't even relax much when he saw the tiny middle-aged Guàlizean lady holding a tray and staring at him with wide eyes.

"Manuela," Ariana said with a smile, but the tiny lady did not smile back. Instead she set the tray down on the side table with a distinct crash before waving a finger under Jack's nose and unleashing a torrent of Spanish so rapid, Ariana was pretty sure he didn't catch more than one word in three.

Which was probably a good thing, considering the names Manuela was calling him for 'defiling her mistress's honor'!

Unable to help herself, Ariana started to giggle. Manuela was half Jack's size; she looked like a terrier trying to scare off a pit bull. The corners of Jack's mouth twitched and she realized he understood more than she thought. He was trying to stave off laughter as well.

"Manuela," she managed to say the housekeeper's name again through her laughter. "This is Captain McAuley. He saved my life."

Manuela's expression did not soften in the slightest as she turned her disapproving glare on Ariana. "I do not care who he is or what he has done, I care about what I just saw! What is your father thinking, to allow him in here?"

"Papi knows I am safe with Jack," Ariana said firmly.

"Your life, perhaps, but apparently not your honor!" Manuela placed her hands on her hips and scowled. "There'll be none of that in this house, missy."

"Uh, Ari?" Jack said when the silence became a little awkward, Manuela glaring at him. "I get the feeling she doesn't like me much."

"Manuela has been our housekeeper since before I was born," Ariana said ruefully, "and I'm pretty sure that I'm still about nine as far as she's concerned."

"If she thinks I'm leaving this room, she'll want to think again," Jack said darkly when Manuela continued to stare at him.

Ariana started giggling, and both of them turned to frown at her when she lost her breath and began to cough.

"Ari, you need to be resting," both Jack and Manuela said at the same moment, in two different languages, before scowling at each other again. Helpless with laughter and coughing, Ariana subsided into the bed and let them fuss over her. By the time she managed to stop coughing, they'd stopped side-eyeing each other and were united in their concern for her, Jack plumping pillows to support her while Manuela brought her a glass of water.

Finally, she felt better and was able to coax Manuela into leaving her alone with Jack, for a little while at least. “I’m in no condition for any of the things you’re worrying about,” she told the housekeeper. “More’s the pity.”

That actually earned her a little snicker from Manuela, and the housekeeper looked Jack up and down. “Can’t say I blame you, Miss Ari,” she threw a parting shot over her shoulder as she left the room. “If I was thirty years younger, I might steal him for myself!”

Ariana had to fight back laughter again, especially when Jack frowned and said disbelievingly “Did she just say what I think she said?”

Ariana’s eyes were sparkling with mirth, shaking fingers pressed to her lips as she looked up at him. She’d never looked more beautiful to Jack. He shook his head at her, sitting back down on the edge of the bed and reaching for her hand.

"Alright, I can tell you're having a damn good laugh at my expense. I don't remember Manuela being here last time?"

She managed to suppress her laughter with a massive effort, and nodded. "She was away. Her daughter had a baby and she was staying with her, while we... took our family holiday."

The holiday which had ended with her mother dead and Ari herself traumatized. Jack nodded soberly.

"And Manuela's been with your family a long time?"

"Before I was born... before Papi and Mama married, even. Manuela cooked and cleaned several apartments in the building where Papi lived, and when he married and bought a house he hired her to keep house for him."

It was a different world to Jack. Raul Monterro was from an old, wealthy family who had once been cattle ranchers and owned huge tracts of the Guàlizean countryside. By the time of Raul's birth, the family's empire was a fraction of what it had once been, but still more than wealthy enough to send Raul to study in England at Eton and Cambridge. Jack had the distinct impression that Raul's family had expected him to go into commercial law or banking, but the young man had confounded expectations by joining the prosecutor's office. Raul's rise through the ranks had been positively meteoric, perhaps partly because of his influential family connections, but in no small part because of his sheer talents, Jack was sure.

Thinking of the way Ariana had grown up, in this big house with servants to see to her every whim, Jack started second-guessing himself. What could he give her? He'd only reached the rank of captain in the army, and while he knew he'd been damn good at his job and he was well suited for the task the Guàlizeans had hired him for, military consultant was hardly a career that would be considered suitable for the consort of the First Daughter. Because everything Jack had heard pointed to Raul becoming President at the next election, little more than a year away now.

"Jack!"

Ariana was waving her hand in front of his face, pulling him back from his glum reverie. He blinked, gave her a weak smile.

"Where were you?" She tilted her head and gave him an appealing smile. "Am I not holding your attention?"

"You always have my full attention. Here, it looks as though Manuela was bringing you some lunch." Rising to his feet, he collected the tray Manuela had left behind. "There's soup of some kind, which you should probably have while it's still warm. Looks like corn?"

"It'll be ajiaco, potato and corn soup. Are there arepas with it?"

Ariana had her appetite back, it seemed, and Jack felt reassured that she was well on the mend as he watched her eat, nibbling on a couple of the arepa corn cakes she insisted he share. There was far more food on the tray than she could possibly eat, and in the end she insisted she was quite satisfied and requested he remove the tray.

“And then come here.” Shifting a little to the side, she held her arms out to him.

“Ari,” he shook his head at her. “You’re in no shape for... well, anything.”

“Jack, I want you to hold me.” Her soft, earnest words stopped his protest dead. “I want to feel your arms around me. I thought you were dead, and it broke me. El Lobo couldn’t break me for all his threats and his guns, even finding out that Tomàs betrayed us and killed Elliot didn’t break me, but thinking you were dead...” she shook her head, tears beginning to spill down her cheeks again, and Jack went to her without thinking, lying down beside her and drawing her into his arms, kissing her forehead and stroking her shining hair.

“Hush,” he whispered. “Hush, angel. I’m here.”

He held her close until her shaking shoulders stilled, and then he spoke.

“It was you who almost died, Ari. I thought I’d lost you when I saw you lying there on the stones, so still, blood all over you.” Jack choked up, barely able to speak. “I was on my knees holding you, begging you not to leave me, when the boat showed up.”

"I met the boat captain, and the paramedics who saved my life," Ariana said quietly against his shirt. "The captain is getting a medal for bravery... he headed for the beach when the helicopter came in. The paramedics told me I'd have bled out before he got there if you hadn't been holding the wounds in my chest and back closed with your bare hands."

Just thinking about it made Jack feel queasy. He raised his hand to place it below her collarbone, remembering with sickening clarity the feel of her blood, slippery on his hands.

"I told you then how much I loved you, even as you were slipping away," he whispered against her forehead, nuzzling the softness of her hair, breathing in the sweet fragrance that was uniquely his Ari. "I'm never letting you go again."

Smiling, Ari nestled closer still, placing her hand over his and holding on tight. "Too damn right you're not," she told him.

Epilogue

With Jack now working in Guàlize and her father finally declaring his candidacy for the Presidency — with the full support of the outgoing incumbent — Ariana's decision to stay in Guàlize wasn't a difficult one. The Santa Maria hospital was more than happy to have her join their staff, though she fought a few battles with her new security team, handpicked by Jack and Ramón Gutierrez, in order to be allowed to actually treat patients. Raul threatened to make her Minister for Health if he won the election.

"Only if you want me to take Jack and disappear back into the jungle," Ariana warned.

Raul chuckled. He had convinced her into accompanying him to a few events in Guàlize City while he was campaigning; with no wife, she understood that he would need her to take on at least some of the duties of a First Lady should he be elected. She grimaced to herself a little. Her kidnapping and the death of El Lobo Negro had only cemented her father's popular support. His closest opponent was twenty points behind in the polls and fading fast. Raul Monterro was going to be Guàlize's thirty-third president and his daughter was just going to have to learn to deal with everything that came along with that office.

Of course, everything was a lot more palatable with Jack present. Ariana's eyes softened as she looked across the room at where he was piling a plate with food from the breakfast buffet. The shorter man at his shoulder laughed as Jack said something, turned around to grin at Ariana. Lieutenant Hunter — former-Lieutenant, he now insisted with his trademark cheeky grin — had arrived in Guàlize less than three weeks after Jack. "Can't leave the Captain down here all alone," he'd said, "last time I did that, he managed to get you shot, Doctor Monterro."

"Fair point," Raul said, and somehow Hunter was assigned to Ariana's security squad temporarily, at least until Jack and Ramón Gutierrez managed to get it filled with men they trusted.

Hunter put a plate piled high with food in front of Ariana now. She gave him a reproachful look, which he ignored.

"You missed dinner last night, assisting in that surgery with Doctor Cardones. Eat up."

She sighed and picked up her fork, a small smile touching her lips. Between Hunter, Jack and her father, she was thoroughly cosseted. Fortunately, she was discovering that she quite liked that.

Jack took his seat beside her, eyes warm as he smiled at her, the scar on his chin tugging his grin crooked. He was still beautiful in her eyes, the man she loved.

"We should get married," Ariana said impulsively.

Jack snorted the sip of coffee he'd just taken back out his nose; Raul and Hunter both started laughing.

"You do know that it's customary for the man to propose, my dear?" Raul asked eventually through his chuckles.

Ariana rolled her eyes at him. "I'd be waiting a long time. Jack's still battling a conviction that he somehow isn't good enough for me because he's a soldier."

"Let's give them the room," Hunter got to his feet, nodded to Raul, who followed him out still chuckling and shaking his head at his daughter's audacity.

"Well, if that's how you feel," Jack had mopped the coffee from his face now, "I've been holding on to something for a while for you."

Ariana watched in astonishment as he slipped from his chair, going to one knee beside her, reaching down to unbutton a pocket of his combat pants. A velvet pouch was produced, and from the pouch he drew a ring, a slim band of gold with a row of tiny diamonds set into a central channel.

"I figured that you wouldn't want anything too bulky or too flashy." The words he'd been struggling with for weeks flowed easily now that Ariana had taken the first huge step for him. Reaching for her left hand, he slipped the ring gently onto her finger. "I'd started looking when your father called me into his office. Said that he already had exactly what I needed."

"It was Mama's," a tear welled in her eye, slipped free to roll down her cheek. Jack put his hand up to thumb it away gently, caressing her cheek.

"I truly wish I'd known her. She must have been one amazing lady, because her daughter's the most incredible woman I've ever met."

Ariana laughed through her tears, lifting both her hands to frame Jack's face in them. "I think you're biased," she told him.

"Of course I am, I'm in love with you."

"I've been in love with you since I was nineteen, Jack. No way am I letting you escape now!" She admired the ring on her finger.

"Shackle me with that ball and chain, angel. I'm more than ready."

Laughing for joy, she threw her arms around his neck and hung on tight as he very satisfactorily kissed her breathless.

THE END

The Rescue Rangers will return in Ranger's Homecoming, when Jason Hunter is called back to the tiny town where he grew up — only to discover that something's very wrong in the remote woods of northern Idaho.

If you enjoyed reading Ranger's Rescue, please consider leaving a review on Amazon, Goodreads or Bookbub, and thank you for taking the time to read!

You can find my web page at caitlynlynch.com. Pay a visit and sign up to my mailing list to be notified of my next scorching hot publication! I also share regular giveaways, tell you about super freebies and new releases from author friends of mine.

(You can unsubscribe at any time, and I promise not to spam you.)

Also By Caitlyn Lynch

RESCUE RANGERS SERIES

RANGER'S RESCUE

RANGER'S HOMECOMING

RANGER'S MISSION

RANGER'S BLOOD

SUNFISH ISLAND RESORT SERIES

FINDING CORY

THE RELUCTANT BILLIONAIRE

HER FAKE ISLAND WEDDING

SLOW SIMMER

FIGHTING FATE

CROP IT LIKE IT'S HOT

STANDALONE BOOKS

IF WISHES WERE HORSES - AN IRISH ROMANCE

CAR CRASH LOVE

KITTENS FOR CHRISTMAS

DANA'S DUO

HOT FOR HEATHER

ELEVATOR ENCOUNTERS SERIES

ELLIE'S ENCOUNTER

JULIET'S ROMEO

THE BEST MAN FOR LEAH

RANGER HEAT SERIES

FIRST SUBMISSION

SECOND SURRENDER

THIRD THRILLS

www.ingramcontent.com/pod-product-compliance
Lightning Source LLC
Chambersburg PA
CBHW020946310726
48980CB00001B/71

* 9 7 8 0 6 4 5 1 8 2 8 6 6 *